P9-ASH-343

MY TEACHER GLOWS IN THE DARK

DON'T MISS THE OTHER BOOKS IN THIS SIZZLING SERIES:

My Teacher Is an Alien

My Teacher Fried My Brains

My Teacher Flunked the Planet

MY TEACHER GLOWS IN THE DARK

Bruce Coville

ALADDIN

NEW YORK LONDON TORONTO SYDNEY NEW DELHI

This book is a work of fiction. Any references to historical events, real people, or real places are used fictitiously. Other names, characters, places, and events are products of the author's imagination, and any resemblance to actual events or places or persons, living or dead, is entirely coincidental.

ALADDIN

An imprint of Simon & Schuster Children's Publishing Division
1230 Avenue of the Americas, New York, NY 10020
This Aladdin edition September 2014
Copyright © 1991 by General Licensing Company, Inc.
Cover illustration copyright © 2014 by Glen Mullaly
All rights reserved, including the right of reproduction in whole or in part in any form.
ALADDIN is a trademark of Simon & Schuster, Inc., and related logo
is a registered trademark of Simon & Schuster, Inc.
For information about special discounts for bulk purchases, please contact Simon & Schuster
Special Sales at 1-866-506-1949 or business@simonandschuster.com.
The Simon & Schuster Speakers Bureau can bring authors to your live event.
For more information or to book an event contact the Simon & Schuster Speakers Bureau
at 1-866-248-3049 or visit our website at www.simonspeakers.com.
Designed by Jessica Handelman
The text of this book was set in Weiss Std.
Manufactured in the United States of America 0714 FFG
2 4 6 8 10 9 7 5 3 1
Library of Congress Control Number 2013958242
ISBN 978-1-4814-0432-7 (hc)
ISBN 978-1-4169-0333-8 (pbk)
ISBN 978-1-4391-1245-8 (eBook)

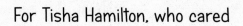

For Tisha Hamilton, who cared

TABLE OF CONTENTS

My Teacher Glows in the Dark

CHAPTER ONE
I CHOOSE THE STARS

So there we were—Susan Simmons, Duncan Dougal, and me, Peter Thompson—sitting in an alien spaceship the size of New Jersey, waiting to learn how we were supposed to save the world, when Susan said, "All right, Peter, give."

"Beg your pardon?" I asked innocently.

"Tell us what's been going on! Five months ago you took off for outer space with Broxholm. Five minutes ago you showed up in a beam of blue light and told Duncan and me we had to help you save the world. I want to know what happened in between."

"Me, too!" said Duncan.

Five months ago I wouldn't have cared what Duncan Dougal thought. As far as I was concerned, he was the world's biggest snotball, a kid whose main hobbies were drooling on his homework, farting in class, and beating me up. I thought he was as likable as a mosquito, as friendly as a rattlesnake, and as useful as a screen door in a spaceship.

But that was before I got a good look at the inside of his head—which was less frightening and more sad than I ever would have guessed.

"Well, since you asked . . . ," I drawled.

"Peter," snapped Susan, "for five months every kid in Kennituck Falls has been dying to know what happened to you after you went off with Broxholm. Stop stalling and tell the story, or you're going to be very sorry!"

So I told them. But that wasn't good enough. Oh, no. Now they insist I have to write it down. "We wrote about our part," they keep saying. "Now it's your turn."

So here goes:

As you probably know, it all started when this alien named Broxholm wanted to kidnap five kids from our sixth grade class last spring. He started by trapping our real teacher, Ms. Schwartz, in a force field. He kept her in his attic while he disguised himself as a substitute teacher named Mr. Smith and took over our class.

One day Susan followed Mr. Smith home and saw him peel off his face. Underneath his human mask was a green-skinned, orange-eyed alien.

Susan came to me for help, mostly because she didn't think anyone else would believe her. She thought *I* might because I used to read so much science fiction.

The two of us spent days trying to figure out how to stop Broxholm. One night I was sitting home alone, eating a can of cold beans and wondering where my father was, when it hit me that if we *couldn't* stop Broxholm, if some kids *had* to go into space, I might as well be one of them. It wouldn't be any worse than staying where I was. And it might be better.

I was frightened by the idea, of course. But I didn't think the aliens were going to dissect my brain or anything like that. In fact, I figured I might learn as much from them as they did from me.

That was the key, I guess; I knew I could learn something. That was important to me, since learning is the one thing I really like. If that sounds strange, look at it like this: if other kids treated you like a nerd and a geek all the time, if you went for weeks feeling like books were your only friends— well, you might really be into learning, too.

Anyway, between being the school dumping ground for emotional toxic waste and having a father who didn't give two bags of llama droppings whether I was alive or dead, I figured I didn't have much to lose by going with Broxholm.

Besides, more than anything else in the world, I wanted to travel to the stars and explore other planets.

That's why when Susan and the school band overpowered the alien on the night of our spring concert, I slipped around back to help him escape.

After I let Broxholm out, he turned and used something that looked like a pencil to *melt* the door shut.

Oh, oh, I thought. *Now you're in for it, Peter.*

But then I thought, *Well, wait a minute. If he has a weapon like that, he could have fried the whole crowd.*

Since he *hadn't,* I figured he wasn't going to make me into sausage; at least, not right away.

So when he started to run, I began to run alongside him.

"What are you doing?" cried the alien.

"I want to come with you!"

I think Broxholm would have stopped running right then, if he had figured it was safe. It wasn't, so he kept going. He was in good shape; I didn't hear him pant or gasp for breath at all. (Of course, for all I knew, when people from his planet got tired it made their armpits ache.)

Three blocks from the school he stopped running.

Then he disappeared.

I felt like my heart had disappeared, too. Never mind that Broxholm was a lean, green kidnapper from outer space. He was going back to the stars, and I wanted to go with him.

"Broxholm!" I yelled. "Wait! Take me!"

"Be quiet while I adjust this!" snapped a voice beside me.

5

An instant later I disappeared, too. Which is to say, I became invisible because of something Broxholm did.

"Wow," I whispered, looking down at where I used to be, "that's *awesome!*"

"Shut up, or you stay here," growled Broxholm.

I shut up. I may have saved his bacon back at the school, and I may have been the only one willing to go with him, but I figured if I got in the way of his escape, Broxholm would dump me faster than my mother had dumped my father when something better came along.

"Now, follow me," whispered Broxholm.

"How? I can't see you!"

After a moment of silence, I felt strong hands grab me by the waist. "Stay quiet!" hissed Broxholm as he tossed me over his shoulder. It reminded me of the first day I had met him, when he picked up Duncan and me to stop us from fighting.

He started to run. He was amazingly fast.

When we reached the little house where Brox-holm had been living, he made us both visible again. Turning to me, he said, "I have some things to do before we can go. I also owe you a favor. Here it is: you have three minutes to change your mind. Otherwise, you're coming with me."

Before I could say a thing, he walked away—leaving me alone to make the biggest decision of my life.

Back at school that decision had been easy. Lying in my bed, in my empty house, I had known for sure what I would do. But this wasn't just some wishing game anymore. It was real.

I thought about my father. Would he miss me? Probably. At least, for a little while. Then he'd probably be just as glad I was gone; one less nuisance for him to cope with.

I thought about school, where I spent most of my time trying not to get beat up by Duncan and other jerks who thought being smart was a crime.

My life would have been a lot different if it was okay to be smart in school. But it's not. It's okay to be pretty smart. But not *real* smart—which is kind of stupid when you think about it. I mean, all these guys picking on smart kids and calling them geeks and dweebs are going to grow up and want to know why *they* don't *do something* about the terrible state the world is in.

I can tell you why. By the time they grow up, most of the kids who really could have changed things are wrecked.

I'll bet you this very minute, even while you're reading these words, some kid who's bright enough to cure cancer when he or she grows up is getting hassled for being an "egghead."

Any takers?

Anyway, I had plenty of reasons to run away. But that wasn't what made up my mind. I didn't just want to run away; I wanted to run *to* something. And that something was space.

I thought about my father again, and wondered if he had ever loved me.

I thought about the stars, and the secrets they held.

Broxholm walked into the kitchen, carrying a large wooden box and two flat pieces of plastic. I recognized the pieces of plastic: they were part of his communication system. Later I found out that the box was his dressing table, all folded up.

"Well?" he asked.

My hands were trembling like a pair of gerbils that had just been dropped into a snake pit. Some of that was terror; some of it was pure excitement. Looking straight into his huge orange eyes, I whispered, "I'm coming with you."

CHAPTER TWO

THE CELLAR
BENEATH THE CELLAR

Broxholm didn't congratulate me, or thank me, or say he was glad to have me along. He just nodded, said, "Follow me," and started toward the cellar door.

The cellar was pretty much as I remembered it from the times I had snuck in with Susan. But Broxholm surprised me. When we reached the far wall, he pressed his hand against a concrete block. A section of the floor tilted back. Blue-gray light streamed up through the opening.

"You first," he said, nodding toward the hole.

Swallowing hard, I approached the light. Then I

looked down, and my fear was washed away in wonder. The trapdoor led to an enormous chamber; in the chamber was a spaceship.

A stairway curved along the side of the chamber. I scrambled down the steps. Broxholm was close behind me.

This second cellar was as polished as the first had been rough. The soft light that filled it came from the wall itself. I say wall because that's all the room had—a single gently curving wall with no edges and no corners. When I put my hand against it, it felt smooth, and slightly warm.

I felt like I was inside an egg.

Still, it was the ship that took most of my attention. Staring at it, I felt such a wave of joy that I thought I might float right off the floor. This was more than my ticket off a planet where I'd never been very happy; it was the key to the stars, and everything I'd dreamed of.

The top of the ship was a half sphere. This rested on a base that looked like a fifty-foot-wide soup bowl surrounded by a ring of lights. The base tapered down in layers, a little like a kid's toy top.

11

Broxholm whistled three harsh notes and an opening appeared in the side of the ship. A long strip of silvery metal stretched down to where we stood. Turning to me, Broxholm said: "Enter."

I stepped onto the silvery plank. It started to move. Feeling as if the ship was about to swallow me, I jumped back.

"Hurry!" snapped Broxholm.

I ran up the plank.

Once inside, I was aching to look around. But Broxholm hustled me to a platform that floated us up to the next level.

"Sit," he said, pointing toward one of four large chairs.

I sat. The padding on the chair was comfortable.

Taking a seat near me, Broxholm pushed a couple of buttons. Part of the curved wall slid aside. He laid his hand on a glowing pad. The ship began to slide forward, into a dark area. Suddenly we started to float. I was afraid we were going to hit the ceiling. But at the last possible moment, Broxholm's *entire back yard* flipped up, like a giant trapdoor.

As we lifted away I saw cop cars racing toward the house. One stopped. The door flew open and a blond kid scrambled out.

"Susan!" I cried.

She couldn't hear me, of course. That didn't stop me from making a fool of myself. Seeing her made me remember that not *everything* down there was rotten. "Wait!" I cried, turning to Broxholm. "Wait. I want to go back!"

Broxholm didn't even look at me as he moved his hands over the control panel. "There's no turning back now," he snapped.

The ship began to move faster. I watched the earth drop away beneath us. Within seconds I had lost sight of Susan, the house, even the town.

I felt hollow inside.

"Stop that," said Broxholm. He shook his head. "You earthlings! You never know what you want. If you'd stop trying to hold on to everything, you'd be a lot happier."

It wasn't until he spoke that I realized I was crying. "Sorry," I whispered, wiping my eyes with the back of my hand.

Broxholm touched my shoulder. "Don't look back," he said softly. "Look up!"

When I did, I started to cry again—this time out of sheer joy. We were heading for the moon. Beyond it lay the void of outer space, a deep black sprinkled with stars.

The moon continued to grow in the viewing space.

"We're going awfully fast, aren't we?" I asked after a moment.

"Compared to what?"

"Well, compared to earth rockets."

"Yes."

The guy was not much of a conversationalist. I was about to ask why the acceleration hadn't pushed me into my seat when we began to make a curve around the moon. When we got to the other side, I was astonished into silence myself.

One problem with writing about aliens is that sometimes it gets hard to describe things. For example, if I say that what I saw now was the biggest thing I had ever seen in my life, that wouldn't be true. A lot of things in nature—like the sun, the moon, and the stars—are bigger.

But if I say it was the biggest man-made thing I ever saw, that wouldn't be true either, because this wasn't made by men—or women, for that matter. It was made by aliens. And it was enormous—a huge lavender sphere that made Broxholm's ship look like an ant on the face of Mount Rushmore.

"What is that?" I finally managed to whisper.

"The good ship *New Jersey*," replied Broxholm.

I blinked. "The *New Jersey*?"

Broxholm pulled on his nose, which stretched out to about twice its normal length, then snapped back into place. I learned later that this is what people on his planet do instead of sighing.

"One of the senior members of our ship's crew has a rather bizarre sense of humor," said Broxholm. "This crew member has also spent a lot of time studying your planet. When the ship was built, it decided that since the ship's surface area was equal to that of New Jersey, that should be the name of the ship. Not everyone was amused."

"The ship decided?" I asked in puzzlement.

"No, the crew member," said Broxholm.

"But you said 'it' decided."

15

"That's because I'm wearing an implant that translates everything I say into English, and no pronoun in your language properly describes this crew member, who is neither a he nor a she, but something else all together."

"What else is there?"

Broxholm pulled on his nose again. "This crewperson comes from a planet where it takes five different genders just to get an egg—and three more to hatch it."

My mind was starting to spin. But before I could ask more questions, a hole opened in the side of the great sphere and a multicolored beam of light extended to our little vessel.

"Docking beam," said Broxholm, pointing to the light. "Soon we'll be inside. Then the fun begins."

"Fun?"

"Sarcasm," said Broxholm softly. "I will have to explain why you are with me. That will not be fun. Not at all."

CHAPTER THREE
THE NAKED STRANGER

Sarcasm? Did that mean Broxholm had a sense of humor? The idea fascinated me. But this didn't seem like the time to ask about it, since I had more important questions in mind—such as, "*Why* won't it be fun?"

"I will tell you later," replied Broxholm. "If I am able. Right now I have business to attend to."

His hands moved swiftly across the control board, which looked like a lot of marbles embedded in a sheet of black concrete. Sometimes he pushed the marbles (or whatever they were), sometimes he rolled them, sometimes he tapped them.

Suddenly a face appeared at the right of the

panel. To my surprise, it didn't look like Broxholm. The forehead was low, the skull wide, the skin a strange shade of yellow.

"Oorbis tiktum?" asked the face.

"Broxholm, requesting emergency landing status. I have one young earthling with me."

I wondered why he spoke in English, until I remembered that his implant forced him to.

Clearly, the alien understood him anyway. "Coopla daktum!" cried the face. Its skin turned orange, and the screen went blank.

"He's not happy, is he?" I said.

"That was a she. And as I was supposed to arrive six hours later, with a total of five children, all of whom were supposed to be asleep, she is naturally somewhat disturbed."

By this time the docking beam had pulled us most of the way in. Imagine you're a flea. Now imagine you're walking through the door of the Empire State Building. That's what it was like for me going into the ship. For a while all I could think was, *This thing is so BIG!* Then my mind did a little flip, and I started thinking, *I'm so SMALL!*

Then I got sort of confused between being afraid and being excited.

Also, I had to go to the bathroom.

The docking beam pulled us into an area that had to be three times as long as a football field. The walls, which were about a thousand feet high, were lined with huge shelves. About half the shelf spaces were filled with spaceships.

None of the ships looked anything like Broxholm's.

When we were about three quarters of the way across this space, the docking beam deposited us on a shelf.

Broxholm did one of his nose-sighs. "Time to face the music," he said.

Given how much Broxholm hated music, that sounded worse coming from him than it would have from anyone else I had ever met. Or was it just his language implant, changing his words into a common English phrase?

I didn't have time to ask, because the top of the ship flipped up, and we began to float into the air. About a meter above the ship, we started to drift in different directions.

"Broxholm!" I cried. "What's going on?"

"We have to be disinfected," he answered, as a hole opened in the wall in front of me.

I struggled, but it was like fighting with air. No matter how I twisted, the invisible beam held me in its grip. Feet first, flat on my back, floating a hundred feet above the floor of the docking area, I was pulled into a small white room shaped a little like an egg that's been stood on end.

"Branna praxim pee-doongie prit," said a musical voice.

I looked around—which didn't take long, since the whole chamber wasn't more than four feet wide. I couldn't see whoever had spoken the words. I couldn't even see a device that the words might have come from.

"Branna praxim pee-doongie prit," repeated the voice gently.

A picture appeared on the wall. It showed an alien—one who looked completely different from Broxholm—standing in a room like this. As I watched, the alien took off its clothes.

I blinked in surprise. Then I remembered the last

thing Broxholm had said to me: "We have to be disinfected."

They wanted *me* to take off *my* clothes!

"Now just a ding-danged minute!" I said.

"Branna praxim pee-doongie prit," said the voice
again.

"Uh-uh. Sorry. I don't do naked in front of
strangers!"

Either whoever was speaking didn't understand
me, or didn't care. A blue beam flashed down from
the ceiling, locking me in place. It was a force
field, just like the one Broxholm had used to keep
Ms. Schwartz a prisoner. I tried to struggle, but I
couldn't even scream. Everything stops when you're
in a force field.

I heard the slightest of noises behind me. I tried
to turn to see what had made it. I couldn't, of course.
The force field held me firm.

Suddenly I felt something tickle down my back.

What was going on?

I heard the same noise in front of me. From the
wall came a tiny ray of light. A laser beam! Starting
at my chin, the laser moved all the way down to my

feet. I couldn't see it all the way down, because I couldn't bend my head. But I could feel that tickle. A few more tickles—down my arms, around my legs, and suddenly the force field disappeared.

I could move again! The only problem was, the instant I did, my clothes all fell off. The laser had sliced my shirt, my pants, my shoes and socks, even my underwear, into pieces—and had done it all without touching my skin.

"Get me out of here!" I yelled. "Get me some *clothes!*"

No answer.

Did that mean there wasn't anyone there? Just as well, I decided, since I didn't have any clothes on. But how long were the aliens going to leave me here? Or was someone watching me even now— watching, but not speaking?

That made sense, in a way. If the alien mission was to study earthlings, then probably they were doing that right now—especially since I was the only one they had.

I decided if I was going to be *the* sample earthling, I was going to do my best not to act like an idiot.

So I began to take deep breaths. I felt myself getting a little calmer. I mean, it wasn't like no one had ever seen me naked before. I've been to the doctor. And next year I would be taking showers in gym class.

Come to think of it, given my choice of getting stuck naked in front of a bunch of aliens, or in a seventh-grade gym class, I'd choose the aliens any day. At least *they* won't flick your butt with a wet towel!

Unfortunately, just as I was getting calm, my little chamber started to fill with gas. Was this a test, to see if I would panic? Were they going to knock me out and do some medical exams?

Or were they going to kill me and dissect me?

I held my breath until my lungs were screaming for air. When I couldn't resist any longer I took a deep, gasping breath.

"Prandit kooma," said the same voice I had heard before.

Weird musiclike sounds began drifting into the chamber. As I felt myself begin to get drowsy, I heard a slight hiss and saw a purple mist filtering down from the ceiling. I wanted to hold my breath

23

again, but I didn't seem to have the willpower.

The music played on. It wasn't like anything you or I would recognize as music, but it was beautiful. My eyelids drooped. Soon I slumped against the side of the chamber and slid to the floor, naked and sound asleep.

CHAPTER FOUR
CROCDOC

When I opened my eyes again, I was lying on a table in a room that was filled with soft green light. I was still naked. A tall alien who looked a little bit like a human crocodile—or at least like a human crocodile would look if it was red instead of green—was standing over me.

"Feeling better?" asked the alien softly.

Actually, what it said was, "Klaakah greebratz?" But my brain *heard* it as "Feeling better?"

I sat up, got dizzy, and lay back down.

"What's going on?" I whispered.

"I just did a little work on your head," said the

alien, as casually as if it was announcing it had gone to the corner for a loaf of bread. "I'm sorry I didn't have a chance to explain the situation before I started, but I hadn't been expecting you."

"What did you do?" I asked, touching my head nervously.

"I installed a Universal Translator in your brain. That's why you can understand me. From now on, you'll be able to understand almost everyone you meet. We all wear them; it makes life quite a bit easier. As I said, I would have explained before I did the work, but there was no way to make you understand. The only being on board who had an implant that would turn his words *into* your language was Broxholm, and he was tied up."

Did the alien mean Broxholm was busy? Or had they really tied him up, as punishment for letting some kids mess up his mission? With aliens, who knew?

"You can probably sit up now," said the brain surgeon. "You just needed a moment to let your head clear."

Moving slowly, I pushed myself to a sitting position.

"Where are my glasses?" I asked.

"Do you need them?" asked the crocodile person, sounding surprised. (I would say the crocodile *man* or the crocodile *woman*, but the truth is, I had no idea which—if either—it was.)

I looked around and blinked in astonishment. I had never seen things so clearly in my life, not even when I was wearing glasses. "What happened?" I cried.

"I thought as long as I was poking around inside your head I might as well fix your eyes."

"Uh—thanks," I said. I probably should have been more enthusiastic; after all, the alien had done me a real favor. But I still wasn't comfortable with the idea that it had been poking around inside my skull without my permission.

On the other hand, being able to see so clearly without my glasses was *wonderful!*

"Thanks!" I said again, this time more sincere.

The red alien smiled—which meant that I got to see about three hundred and forty-two teeth—and said, "Don't mention it."

I heard a sound behind me. Turning, I saw

another alien, though I couldn't spot the door he had come in by. He was short—probably not more than three feet tall—blue and bald. He had big eyes, a large nose, and a thick white mustache. He also had spindly arms and a potbelly. He was wearing nothing but a pair of baggy red shorts covered with pictures of jumping yellow fish.

I had seen aliens who were frightening, aliens who were strange, and aliens who were almost indescribable. This was the first one I had met who was *cute*.

"Greetings, Peter," said the newcomer. "My name is Hoo-Lan."

Actually, what he said was, "Grrgn ryxkzin, Peter, prrna-prrna Hoo-Lan." But with my new implant I knew exactly what he meant.

His ears flapped as he spoke. To my surprise, I understood that this was his version of a smile—which meant that my language implant translated not only words, but gestures and expressions. When you think about how much of what you mean is carried not by your words, but by your body, that makes sense. It's just not the kind of stuff they usually teach you in French class.

"How are you feeling?" he asked.

I thought about his question for a moment.

"I feel fine," I said finally.

The blue alien gave me another ear flap. "I'm pleased to hear that," he said, in his own language. "As you probably suspect, in addition to receiving a language implant, you have been disinfected. We had to disinfect both you and Broxholm before we could allow you to enter the main body of the ship. That was why he could not be with you when you had your operation, for which you have our apologies."

I was a little surprised to hear him apologize. It was also nice to know that the reason no one had told me what was going on when I first got here was that they just couldn't communicate with me yet.

"Can I stand up?" I asked, turning to the crocodile person.

"If you feel like it."

When I stopped to think about it, I realized that I felt terrific. Had the croc/doc tinkered with the rest of my systems, too? I decided not to ask.

"You wouldn't by any chance have some clothes I could wear, would you?" I asked.

Nose twitching, Hoo-Lan brought his hand from behind his back and tossed me a package wrapped in shiny black material. "I thought you might want these," he said. "Especially since it's time for us to visit the captain."

The package contained my clothes, which were in perfect condition. "I don't get it. I thought these had been lasered into pieces."

"These are computer recreations," said Hoo-Lan. "We put the disinfected scraps of what you had been wearing into the synthesizer. It analyzed fabric and design, then spit out a new set. These are identical to your originals, except that they are stain proof, and almost impossible to tear. If you wish, you can design your own clothes later."

That was interesting. I had never cared much about clothes. But if I could just tell the computer what I wanted, it might be fun to try a few different styles!

Once I was dressed I turned to the CrocDoc, as I now thought of him, and thanked him again for what he had done.

He tapped his elbows together three times.

According to my implant, this meant he was glad to have been of service, and he hoped that he would never have to eat my children.

Let me tell you, this multicultural stuff can keep a guy on his toes!

"Follow me," said Hoo-Lan.

I nodded to CrocDoc, and got ready to follow Hoo-Lan out of the room. The only thing we needed now was a door.

The little alien walked to a place where the wall was marked by a large circle. Next to the circle were twelve rows of multicolored marbles. Hoo-Lan tapped six of the marbles, and the area inside the circle turned blue.

"Step through," he said, gesturing toward the circle.

"Through the wall?" I asked nervously.

"It's not a wall," he replied, giving me a little shove. "It's a transcendental elevator."

"Hey!" I shouted, thinking I was going to smash my face against the circle.

To my surprise, I stepped right *through* the circle. As I did, my whole body began to tingle. The tingling

31

got stronger and stronger. It reminded me of the "pins and needles" you get when your leg falls asleep. Only this was all over my body, and it kept getting stronger.

I wanted to shout, only I couldn't, because I had no mouth. But then, I didn't have hands, feet, or a head, either.

CHAPTER FIVE
THE CRYSTAL CAPTAIN

As quickly as it began, it was over, and I found myself—all of myself—standing in a room that looked like it had been carved out of the inside of a diamond. Hoo-Lan was next to me.

"What happened?" I whispered.

Hoo-Lan looked at me in surprise. "Did you feel something?"

I nodded. He frowned, which meant the same for him as it does for us. "You shouldn't have," he said. "We'll have to look into this."

"But what happened?" I repeated.

"The elevator took you apart and put you back together."

"WHAT?"

"Don't worry—the same thing happened to me. That's how a transcendental elevator works; it breaks you into packets of energy, sends you to another place, then puts you back together."

"Wouldn't it be easier to walk?" I asked, patting myself in various places to make sure I was all there.

Hoo-Lan gave me his version of a shrug. "It's over a hundred miles from the doctor's room to the captain's cabin."

"Oh, well in that case, sure, just send my molecules," I said, wondering if the sarcasm would translate.

"We did," said Hoo-Lan, sounding quite serious. "And now it is time for us to meet the captain."

A tinkle of music played around me. "Indeed it is," translated my language implant.

I turned in a circle, trying to find the source of the sound. "Where did that come from?" I whispered.

Hoo-Lan gestured to a clear tank that stood at one end of the chamber.

"What is it?" I asked.

"The captain."

"Come here, young earthling," said the tank.

I glanced at Hoo-Lan. He nodded, so I crossed to the tank, which looked like a huge, round aquarium. Except there weren't any fish or plants inside. A pair of cables ran from the bottom of the tank into the floor.

"Look more closely," said the voice.

I stared into the tank. After a few seconds I saw a collection of crystals, sharp-edged and many-faceted. It took me a few more seconds to realize that the shapes were slowly moving.

"This is our captain," said Hoo-Lan, adding a name for which there was no translation.

"But how . . . ?"

A sigh tinkled around me. "You carbon-based life forms are so molecular-centric. Until you meet another form of life, you seem convinced that carbon is the only way to grow."

"Sorry," I said. "I didn't mean to offend you."

The air around me filled with a sound like chimes; the implant told me this was laughter.

35

"Hoo-Lan," sang the crystal captain, "I need only speak to Peter. You may leave if you wish."

"I have things to do," said Hoo-Lan, nodding to me. "I will see you soon." As he turned and headed for the transcendental elevator the captain's voice said, "You do realize, my young friend, that you have created a problem for us?"

I blinked. "What's the problem?"

"In a word, *you*. By galactic law, no person of Earth is allowed on board this vessel."

"I thought Broxholm was supposed to bring back *five* of us," I said, feeling somewhat puzzled.

"For observation and analysis only. Any memory of the experience would have been erased from your minds before we returned you to Earth."

"Did you ever wonder how we might feel about that?"

"Not particularly. If I had, it wouldn't have mattered. Except for our fact-finding mission, the Interplanetary Council has banned all contact with the people of Earth. This is the first time in a thousand years this has happened, by the way."

"You mean it's the first time in a thousand years

Earth has been isolated?" I asked, wondering if the aliens had visited a lot in the past.

"It's the first time in a thousand years *any* planet has been isolated."

I didn't like the sound of that. "Should we be honored?" I asked, sounding more smart-alecky than I intended.

"Terrified might be more appropriate."

"Terrified?" I squeaked. The very fact that the captain *said* I should react that way came close to creating the feeling in me.

The captain's voice chimed around me, louder than before. "Earth is the greatest danger faced in the three thousand year history of the Interplanetary League. It appears to be a planet in the grip of mass insanity. We must find out why you kill each other with such reckless abandon."

The language implant was translating what the captain sang into words. But the very sound of the music filled me with fear, and with sorrow.

The crystals in the bottom of the tank shifted. "There is something very strange about your world," continued the captain. "On every other planet where science has developed, the process has taken much longer than it has on Earth. Always before, people ready to enter space have been civilized in a way you humans have avoided altogether."

The captain paused, then sang sadly, "We fear if the people of Earth are allowed into space in their uncivilized state, the results could be disastrous beyond anything you can imagine."

"Allowed?" I asked nervously.

"Allowed. At the moment, we are considering a permanent quarantine on Earth. No one gets on, no one gets off. We don't mind you exploring your own solar system; there's not much there anyway. But we cannot allow you to carry this sickness, whatever it is, into the galaxy at large."

I wanted to cry; for years I had been dreaming of meeting people from another planet. When I finally do meet some, what do I find? *My* planet has embarrassed itself in front of the entire galaxy! I felt like an interstellar geek.

"Of course, quarantine is only one option," said the captain, interrupting my thoughts.

"What else is there?" I asked, more nervous than ever.

"I would rather not say. After all, the teacher does not necessarily discuss all options with the student."

I wondered if the captain really meant "with the enemy." But I couldn't think of a way to say it that didn't sound snotty.

"Anyway," continued the captain, "you can see that your presence here creates a problem."

"Are you going to lock me up?"

The bells that filled the air seemed to sigh. "You see? Only an earthling would think of something like that so quickly. I suppose if you persisted in causing trouble, we might lock you up. But that's just not something we do. However, we do have to decide what we *will* do with you. So tell me, what is it that brought you here? What do you want?"

"To *learn*," I said fiercely.

"Admirable. However, you must realize that the more you learn, the less likely it is we can ever let you return home."

"I don't care about home. I want to see the stars."

"You could have seen them from your own back-yard."

"I want to visit other planets. I want to explore the galaxy. I want to find out what it's all about!" I cried, suddenly realizing I might be the only human ever to have that chance.

"Then you are welcome to join us. You will be assigned to Hoo-Lan, who has been specializing in Earth studies of late."

"How is Broxholm going to feel about that?" I asked, though for all I knew Broxholm never wanted to see me again.

"That's not an issue," said the captain. "Broxholm has other matters to which he must attend. As do I, my new crewmember. Which means that you must leave now. The elevator will take you to your cabin."

Feeling a trifle nervous, I headed for the circle where we had come in. When I glanced back, the captain's tank had changed color. I heard the word for "Farewell" chime through the air as I stepped through the wall.

I didn't feel anything this time, none of the tear-ing sensation that had scared me so much on my first trip through the transcendental elevator. So I figured Hoo-Lan had adjusted the mechanism for me. But the place the elevator delivered me to was so dark I was afraid the thing had malfunctioned.

My heart began to pound. What if it had sent me someplace where no one would be able to find me, some neglected storage space or something? Rooms on this ship didn't even have doors! If I got stuck in a place like that I might die before anyone found me.

I was about to scream for help when a blue light began to glow behind me.

CHAPTER SIX
HOO-LAN

I spun around and found myself face to face with Hoo-Lan.

Well, face to face isn't quite right; given how short he was, it was more like navel to face. Anyway, he was the source of the light. And I mean that exactly. The little alien wasn't carrying a lamp or a flashlight or anything. *He* was glowing—a soft, gentle glow that seemed to come from every square inch of his skin.

"For heaven's sakes, Peter," said Hoo-Lan quietly, "don't be so skittish."

It took me a moment to realize that the words

were spoken in perfect English. I stared at him in surprise. "I didn't know you could speak my language."

"There's a lot about me that you don't know, and a great deal that I have to tell you. That's why I arranged to have you sent here, instead of your own room. I needed a place where we could speak in relative secrecy."

"Secrecy?" I asked nervously.

"Great things are happening," said Hoo-Lan, glancing from side to side. "Power is shifting, and ancient mysteries are being unraveled." His glow seemed to grow more intense. His voice, and his words, sent a chill down my spine.

"What does that have to do with me?" I asked in a whisper.

"Nothing, and everything. Remember, information travels fast, if you know how to grease its skids." He paused, then added, "I'm not sure that made sense."

"Why are we here?" I asked, trying to get him back on track. "*Where* are we, for that matter?"

"In a storage space in the lower third of the good

43

ship *New Jersey*, which at the moment is heading past the planet you call Jupiter."

That scared me. The last spacecraft Earth sent past Jupiter had taken years to get there. We must be moving at an incredible rate! On the other hand, it was a straight answer. Shooting for two in a row, I asked, "What did you bring me here to tell me?"

Hoo-Lan motioned toward a box, indicating I should sit. In the light emanating from his body, I could see that the room was filled with containers of all shapes, sizes, and colors.

I sat. Hoo-Lan scrambled up next to me. Reaching into a pocket in his baggy shorts, he pulled out a black box about half the size of a paperback book.

"You rat," he said, handing it to me.

"What did I do?" I asked, feeling hurt.

Hoo-Lan blinked. "What did you . . . ? Oh, you misunderstood me. I didn't call *you* a rat. *This device* is a URAT—a *U*niversal *R*eader *A*nd *T*ranslator. Press your thumb against the top corner."

I did as Hoo-Lan said. The box opened, pretty much the way a book would if it was only made of two very thick pages. Except the URAT was now stiff, as if it had never been closed.

"This will be your primary information source," said Hoo-Lan. "It contains a small library of important data for navigating your way around the ship. Also a complete listing of crew members. Now, please tell it your name."

"My name is—"

"Wait, wait! I think you need a new name."

"What's wrong with the one I've got?" I asked, feeling a little annoyed. I don't know why I was annoyed. Peter Thompson was nothing special as names go. Heck, the Thompson part came from my father, and I was as glad to be rid of him as he was to be rid of me. No loss there. As for my first name, it was mostly something people used to get my attention when they wanted to tease me. So a new name shouldn't have been any big deal. Still, I had had this one all my life, and I felt somewhat attached to it.

"There's nothing *wrong* with your old name," said Hoo-Lan patiently. "It's just that it's part of your old life. New life, new name, I always say. I shall call you

Krepta, which in the language of my world means 'Child of the Stars.' This is a good name for you, since you are a boy without a planet."

I felt my stomach twist. "A boy without a planet" sounded terribly lonely.

I hesitated. "My name is Krepta," I whispered into the URAT. "Child of the Stars."

"Greetings, Krepta," replied the URAT. "How may I be of service?"

I looked at Hoo-Lan.

"Tell it you wish to travel," he said.

"Where do you wish to go?" asked the URAT, after I had followed Hoo-Lan's advice.

"Actually, I would like something to eat," I said.

"Wise choice," said Hoo-Lan. "Biologically sound, too. When you get to a new place, always find out where to eat and where to hide."

"Will I need to hide here?" I asked nervously.

Hoo-Lan shrugged. I would have pursued the question, but the URAT had started beeping. Looking at it, I saw a pattern of colored dots. It was the same pattern I had seen next to the transcendental elevator. Suddenly some of the dots began to flash.

"It's displaying the destination code," said Hoo-Lan. "When you want to go somewhere, ask the URAT for the code. Punch the code into the control pad beside any elevator, and it will take you to your destination."

"Can I go anywhere I want?"

"Of course," said Hoo-Lan. "Why not?"

"Well, don't you have rules—you know, security precautions against spies, things like that?"

"You have to stop thinking as if you were still on Earth, Peter. We're not the same as you are. I'm the closest thing to a spy on this ship. Certainly the biggest troublemaker."

I looked at him in alarm. "Are you going to get *me* in trouble?" I asked nervously.

"Oh, probably. Anyone who tries to do something worthwhile gets in trouble now and then, don't you think?"

To tell you the truth, I didn't know what to think. I decided to get some more information, and do the thinking later. "What do you mean, you're the closest thing to a spy?" I asked. "Are you a spy, or aren't you?"

"Merely a representative of a minority point of view. As you know, your planet is currently the focus of a great debate. At the moment, I am on the losing side of that debate."

"What side is that?"

Before Hoo-Lan could answer, I heard another beeping. Reaching into his pocket, he took out a second URAT. When he opened it, a face that looked like it belonged to a purple frog appeared on its surface and said, "You are wanted for an urgent meeting."

"The main problem with these things," said Hoo-Lan, tucking away his URAT and hopping down to the floor, "is that they're great for communication, but lousy for privacy. I'm sorry, Krepta, but I can't ignore this call. We'll talk more later. For now, why don't you get something to eat. I'll catch up with you in a while."

He crossed to the wall and started to punch a code into the elevator buttons. Then he stopped, turned to me, and said, "Since you can't see in the dark, maybe you'd better go first."

That made sense. When Hoo-Lan left he would

take my only source of light—namely, himself—with him.

I stepped up to the wall. My URAT was still flashing the code for a dining area, the image of the buttons lighting up in a certain order, pausing, and then repeating the sequence.

I watched the code twice, then punched it into the control pad. Taking a deep breath, I stepped through the wall—and into the middle of a fight.

CHAPTER SEVEN

LUNCH WITH FLEEF AND GURK

"It was a bad idea from the beginning!" said an alien who looked something like a tall brown pickle with arms.

"Nonsense!" snapped the orange alien standing next to him. "A few hours wouldn't have made the slightest bit of difference to those creatures."

This second alien was only a little taller than me, and clearly female, at least by Earth standards. Though her skin was orange, her features were basically human—well, except for the fact that she had a thumb-thick green stalk rising from the top of her head. The stalk ended in a thick knob, which I took to be a sense organ of some sort, since it was constantly rotating. Every once in a while it would stop moving and go, "Neep! Neep!"

"Ah, look!" cried the orange alien, when she noticed me standing there. "We can ask him!"

"It might be nice if we greeted him first," said the pickle.

"Flog me for an oaf!" cried the orange one. "I just get too excited sometimes." Turning to me, she said, "You are the Earth child, are you not?"

Her voice was sweet and gentle.

"I used to be," I replied. "Now I'm a child of the stars."

The orange alien nudged the pickle. "What did I tell you, Gurk. It doesn't matter!"

Gurk squeezed one of the warty things that covered his pickly skin. It popped, releasing a terrible smell.

My implant told me this was his way of saying "Nonsense!"

"Euuuw!" cried the orange alien. "I told you not to do that!" The stalk on the top of her head flopped backward. "Neep," it whispered. "Neee—"

I looked at the alien in alarm, worried that the knob might be permanently disabled, or even dead. But she seemed more annoyed than concerned.

Gurk put his hands on top of his head, which was a gesture of apology. "Sorry, I got carried away. But I still think you're mistaken. Let's start this conversation over, or we'll give the young one a bad impression."

He turned to me. I got ready to hold my breath, in case he was going to communicate by smell again. But his voice was quiet, and when I looked at him more carefully, I realized that he had the kindest, warmest eyes I had ever seen.

Putting his skinny arms together in front of him, he said, "Young one, my name is Gurk. My companion is called Fleef."

"Greetings," said Fleef, who was trying to get the stalk on her head to stand up again.

"Greetings," I replied.

They both looked at me expectantly. "And your name?" asked Gurk, after a moment of silence.

"Oh, I'm sorry. My name is—" I hesitated. Was I Peter Thompson—or was I Krepta?

The aliens were staring at me. I had a sense that they were beginning to wonder if I was stupid.

"My name is Krepta!" I said defiantly.

As I said it, I felt something twist inside me. I had let go of my name and my home, and though I had a new name, and a new home, neither one of them felt like they were really mine.

I wondered if they ever would. I almost said, "Wait, I made a mistake! My name is Peter!"

But that would have been a lie. I wasn't Peter anymore. Hoo-Lan had been right. I was a boy without a planet, and the name I had carried away from Earth no longer fit me.

"Krepta!" said Gurk in surprise. "A Child of the Stars, indeed. And what happened to the name you were born with?"

"I am a different person now," I said softly.

"Well, Krepta," said Fleef, "come and sit with us while we eat. Perhaps you can help us settle a disagreement."

I wasn't sure I wanted to eat with the two of them. Still, if I was going to get along on this ship, I did need to start making friends.

"I'd be glad to eat with you," I said, hoping neither one of them was going to eat something so gross I would get sick just watching them swallow it.

"Are you touchable?" asked Gurk.

I raised an eyebrow. His translator must have interpreted the movement, because he answered the question before I could put it into words.

"Some beings like to be touched, others are deeply offended by certain kinds of contact," he explained, his wonderful eyes looking straight into mine. "If touch does not bother you, then I would put my arm around your shoulder, or place a hand on the back of your neck, to guide you to the sitting place. But it is best to ask, first."

I hesitated. My father wasn't much of a hugger. So the only person who had touched me much back home was Duncan Dougal, and that was only to punch me. Since I wasn't used to it, I was a little nervous about having Gurk touch me, especially with that pickly skin of his. On the other hand, this was a new world, a new life. . . .

"It's okay," I said. "You can touch me."

I thought about adding something about being

careful *where* he touched me, but he had been so worried about offending me at all, I decided it wasn't going to be a problem.

Besides, even though I hadn't gone three steps past the elevator, I could see a whole room full of people just beyond Fleef and Gurk. So I figured I was safe for the time being—at least, as safe as a kid can be in a room where he's the only person who looks more than vaguely human.

Taking me by the arm, Gurk led me to a table at the edge of the room. "There are many beings interested in you," he whispered, "so there's no need to draw too much attention to yourself right now."

"For once we agree," said Fleef.

"Neep!" said the thing on top of her head. I noticed the stalk was standing up straight again.

I also noticed that the room was sort of dim. I was a little puzzled about this, until I decided they had probably set the light at a level most comfortable for the greatest number of different beings.

"Where do we get our food?" I asked.

"Right here!" said Fleef, gesturing to the table.

The table was round, with a smooth black top.

In front of each of us was a set of buttons much like the ones beside the transcendental elevators.

"Do we use these to order?" I asked, pointing to the buttons.

"See, I told you they weren't stupid!" said Gurk.

"Intelligence and emotion are not always connected," replied Fleef. Her orange skin grew darker as she spoke, which my translator informed me was a sign that she was irritated.

"Could you tell me what this is all about?" I asked, trying not to do anything that was going to offend either one of them.

"Later," said Gurk. "First let's order. Have you programmed in any meals yet?"

I shook my head, trusting Gurk's implant to translate the gesture.

"All right, then we'll have to show you how. You are a carbon-based life form, if I remember correctly?"

I nodded, wondering what they would feed me if I wasn't.

"All right, first you punch in your personal code—"

"But I don't have a personal code," I interrupted.

"Gurk," said Fleef gently, "let *me* show him how."

Gurk slid some warts around, which was his way of sighing, and sat back in his chair while Fleef showed me how to find my personal code. Then she helped me tell the master computer the kinds of things that I would like. It took a while, because the food synthesizer wasn't programmed for an earthling. But by asking careful questions, she was able to help me come up with a menu that we both felt would (a) not kill me and (b) not make me throw up.

We all punched in the codes for our meals at the same time. Within seconds a hole opened in the top of the table. Three plates floated out and positioned themselves in front of us.

Gurk's plate had a steaming, writhing mess of something that looked like it wanted to crawl across the table and say hello to me.

Fleef's dinner looked like blue marbles and smelled like rotten eggs mixed with toe jam.

The stuff on my plate actually looked pretty good. That was because Fleef had showed me how to program color and shape into my order. While it didn't taste quite as good as it looked, at least most of it was edible. The only thing I couldn't get down was the stuff that looked like french fries but tasted like peanut butter mixed with rotten blueberries.

While we ate, Fleef told me how to refine my next order, based on what I did and didn't like in this batch of stuff. She was a good teacher, and I was starting to like her.

After we had all had a bit to eat, Gurk said, "Here's the question we were arguing about when you stepped out of the elevator. What would happen if—"

Before he could finish, the lights blinked three times. "Better lie down, Krepta," said Fleef, throwing herself to the floor. "You'll be less likely to throw up that way."

CHAPTER EIGHT

FASTER THAN LIGHT

I stretched out on the floor beside Fleef and Gurk. After a second, I raised my head. Almost everyone else in the large room was on the floor with us.

"Put your head down," whispered Fleef. "Quickly!"

I felt like I was in one of those stories where the king was about to come by, and everyone had to bow down. I stared at the ceiling, wondering if the aliens had some supreme high commander they treated like a god.

At first, I thought the ceiling was made of green marble. Then I noticed that the swirls of color were slowly moving. I was thinking how pretty it was when an ear-splitting squeal sliced through the room, as if some monstrous claw had just scraped across the blackboard of the universe. A low moan rose from the aliens on the floor, the kind of sound you might hear if a thousand kids all began to feel carsick at the same time.

It took me a moment to realize that my own voice was part of that mass moan. My stomach lurched. I clutched at it, trying to keep down what I had eaten. I didn't want to disgust my new friends by throwing up on them! (I was also hoping they were not going to throw up on me. I was pretty nervous about what it might smell like if Gurk tossed his cookies—or whatever it is that giant pickles toss when they lose their lunches.)

Suddenly I felt like I was being pulled apart. Only this was a thousand times worse than my first trip through the transcendental elevator. It was as if some giant had my head, another had my feet, and they were having a tug of war—with about a thousand other people pulling at the top, bottom, and sides of me just for the heck of it.

About the time I thought I absolutely couldn't stand it any longer, it stopped. I lay flat for a moment, wondering what had just happened to me.

Gurk touched my shoulder. "Are you all right, Krepta?" he asked softly.

I was so disoriented it took me a moment to realize he was speaking to me. "I'm not sure," I whispered. "What just happened?"

"The ship made a space-shift," said Fleef softly. "Galactically speaking, it's the only way to travel."

I opened and closed my eyes a few times. The ceiling didn't seem so pretty anymore. In fact, it was kind of nauseating. I wished it would stop moving.

"What's a space-shift?" I asked weakly.

"Instant transportation," said Gurk, rolling over and pushing himself up with his skinny arms.

"Like the transcendental elevators, but on a grand scale," added Fleef. She was already on her feet, holding out a six-fingered orange hand to help me up. "The ship just moved several light-years from where it was when you joined us."

I felt an unexpected sense of loss wash over me. How far from home was I now?

"Could you tell me a bit more?" I asked.

"Well, do you know about the speed of light?" asked Gurk.

"It goes 186,000 miles per second," I said, trusting their implants to figure out what miles are. "It's the fastest thing we know."

"It's the fastest thing *anyone* knows," said Fleef, patting her stalk to make sure it was all right. "Now that would make traveling around the galaxy nearly impossible, since even at the speed of light it would take you years to get from one star system to another. Centuries, sometimes."

"So the best method is to skip all that traveling," said Gurk, sliding a wart across his forehead. "Which is what we just did."

I staggered to my chair, trying to keep my stomach from providing a review of everything I had just eaten. "Could you make that a little more clear?"

Gurk punched some buttons on the food preparation device. A plate floated up, carrying a thick red noodle that had to be at least three feet long.

"How can you eat so soon after that shift?" asked Fleef.

"This isn't a snack, it's a demonstration," replied Gurk. "Sit down, Krepta, and I will try to explain." He picked up the noodle. "If you stretch out this *bee-ranga*—which, by the way, is the preferred snack on the planet Hopfner—you have a straight line. Now, if you were at one end, and the place you wanted to go was at the other end, you would have to travel the entire length of the *bee-ranga* to get there, right?"

I nodded.

"But if you join the ends of the *bee-ranga*, like this, all you would have to do is go from here—to here!" And with that he brought the two ends of the noodle together.

"What does that have to do with us?" I asked.

"That's how this ship travels. We bring two parts of space together and then step across them."

"It's the stepping across that's the hard part," added Fleef. "It makes most beings quite queasy."

"But how do you *do* it?"

"I don't know how it works," said Gurk. "All I know is the basic idea."

That seemed strange, until I thought about how

many people on Earth ride around in cars without having the slightest idea of how they work. I decided to switch questions. "If we just jumped several light-years, then where are we now?"

"How do you expect us to know?" asked Gurk, popping the *bee-ranga* into his mouth. "We're not the captain."

The sight of Gurk eating seemed to make Fleef queasy. "If my friend were feeling a little more polite," she whispered, "he would mention that you could find out by asking your URAT. I would guess we're heading back toward the center of the galaxy. If that was a typical jump, we probably moved about twenty light-years."

A strange feeling came over me. *The fastest rocket ever built on earth couldn't get this far in a hundred years*, I thought to myself.

With a shock, I realized I was homesick.

Fleef tapped me on the shoulder. "Are you all right, Krepta?"

"What? Oh, sure," I lied. "I'm fine, just fine."

I figured there was no point in telling them how I felt. To begin with, I wasn't sure I understood it myself.

Besides, years of living with my father had taught me not to bother talking about things that upset me.

"Good," said Fleef. "Then maybe I can finally ask you my question. What we were arguing about when you first met us was whether or not it made any difference if we borrowed some of your planet's children for a while."

"You mean like when Broxholm was planning to steal some kids from our school?" I asked.

"No, no, no," said Fleef. "We weren't going to steal anyone—just borrow them for a while. It's part of a research project. We would have brought them back! Which is why I don't think anyone would have minded that much. But Gurk says people, parents especially, would have been terribly upset. So—which of us is right?"

"Gurk is. Parents would have gone berserk. You can't just go around stealing—er, *borrowing* kids like that."

"See!" said Gurk triumphantly. Actually, he didn't say it, he pulled off one of his brown warts and waved it in front of Fleef's face, which my translation device told me was a sign of victory.

"But it doesn't make sense," said Fleef. She looked upset. Not just unhappy because Gurk had won the argument; she seemed genuinely disturbed.

"What doesn't make sense?" I asked.

"Oh, ignore her," said Gurk. "She's just annoyed because she wants to believe you people don't have well developed emotions."

"Why would you want to believe that?" I asked.

Fleef didn't answer. Gurk spoke for her. "Because then she won't feel so bad if we have to blow up your planet."

CHAPTER NINE
ROOM SERVICE

If you've ever just missed being in some terrible car accident, you know what I felt like. My hands were trembling, my heart was pounding, and my stomach wasn't sure where it wanted to go.

"You want to do what?" I whispered, staring at Fleef in horror.

The stalk on her head was whirling around like crazy, the little knob going "Neep neep neep!" as if someone was trying to catch and kill it. According to my implant this was a sign of extreme emotional distress.

Tough! I thought. *Your distress can't be any worse than mine.*

Sure, I'd had my problems with Earth. But these guys were talking about blowing up billions of human beings, including my father, Ms. Schwartz, Susan Simmons—and *you.*

"You'd better go, Krepta," said Gurk, touching my arm.

"No! I want to know what this is all about."

Gurk rearranged a few warts, a signal that the topic was definitely closed. I decided leaving was a good idea after all. If I wasn't going to get any more information, I needed some time and some privacy to think about what I had just heard.

As I pushed myself away from the table, Fleef reached out and touched my arm. "Please do not take this personally, Krepta. We will discuss it more later."

I looked at her in astonishment. "You want to blow up my planet, and I'm not supposed to take it personally?" I asked.

Shaking with fury, I stalked away from the table.

At the transcendental elevator I asked the URAT

to give me the code for my room. At once a pattern flashed on the screen. I punched it into the keypad, stepped through the elevator, and found myself in an egg-shaped space. Its curving wall was a soft brownish-orange color. Since there were no doors or windows, it really felt like being inside an egg.

I liked the color and the shape of the room. Unfortunately, it was completely bare, with not a stick of furniture to be seen.

Broxholm's house had been bare of furniture, too. Was that the alien style? Did they expect me to just sit on the floor, staring at the walls?

It's interesting how much little things can distract you when you have something big on your mind. What I wanted to do was worry about the fate of the Earth. What I found myself fretting about was the fact that I didn't have a chair to sit and worry in.

I decided to ask the URAT. Flipping open the box, I said, "Can I have some furniture?"

"Certainly," replied the mechanical voice.

"Well, how do I get it?"

"All you need to do is ask."

"I'm asking."

"You have to specify what you want."

"What kind of choices do I have?" I asked, trying not to sound too impatient.

"We have an enormous variety of personal convenience items on file," said the URAT. "You can also design your own. The possibilities are infinite."

"Is there a way to know what you have on file?"

Instantly the wall in front of me began to display a picture. That was neat; the entire wall was like a giant television screen—except that the image was clearer than any television you have ever seen.

The picture it showed now was actually a chart, with all kinds of furniture on it—and I do mean all kinds. Not only did it show chairs, desks, and beds, it had items that looked like everything from medieval torture devices to toilets designed for octopi.

Which reminded me: "Is there a bathroom attached to this room?"

"No."

"Then how am I supposed to go to the toilet?" I cried, suddenly feeling desperate.

"There are many bathrooms available, simply none attached to this room, Krepta."

That made sense. After all, if a transcendental elevator could move you from one place to another instantly, there was no need to have your bathroom actually *attached* to your room. It could be fifty miles away, and it wouldn't make any difference. Maybe you didn't even *have* your own bathroom; for all I knew, the elevator just sent you to the first empty bathroom it found.

"Give me the code for a bathroom, please," I said to the URAT.

"Insufficient data."

"What do you mean?" I cried, crossing my legs.

"I do not know what kind of bathroom you need. We have fifty-three different types of facilities."

I remembered the octopi toilets, or whatever they were, that I had seen on the first chart. Given the variety of aliens I had met already, it made sense that the ship needed a lot of different bathrooms.

"I'm glad I'm not the plumber for this place," I muttered.

"Yes," agreed the URAT, "that would be a disaster."

"Look, I don't need to be insulted by a machine. Just tell me how to find a bathroom!"

The URAT informed me that it needed to know more about me. After it had asked fifteen or twenty questions, some of them very personal, it finally gave me a bathroom code.

Not a moment too soon! I thought, as I punched the code into the control pad. I stepped into a bathroom that was only mildly odd—which is to say that it only took me about five minutes (five desperate minutes) to figure out how to use it.

When I was done, I returned to my own room. The furniture chart was still on the wall. I wondered if it only showed available *categories* of furniture, since there was only one chair, one desk, one octopus's toilet, and so on.

"Can you show me other chairs?" I asked.

Instantly, the image changed to a chart that held over fifty different kinds of chairs.

"Can I have one of those?" I asked, pointing to a comfortable looking armchair.

"Color?" asked the URAT.

"What do you have?"

A chart with about a hundred colors appeared on the wall. After I chose one I liked, the URAT asked about size.

Size? Chairs are chairs, right?

Not when you're on a ship the size of New Jersey, filled with who knows how many varieties of aliens.

By the time I was done answering questions, we had designed a chair that was as perfectly matched to me as a handmade suit would have been. This was neat!

What was even neater was that after I finally gave the URAT all the information it requested I heard a humming noise. Less than five minutes later the very chair I had ordered popped through the door of the transcendental elevator.

This was the ultimate in home shopping!

Plunking down in my chair, I tried to think. From what Fleef and Gurk had said, while some aliens wanted to blow up the Earth, no definite decision had been made yet.

Even so, it was clear that the planet was in danger. Only I got the feeling that since I had abandoned Earth, no one expected me to care.

But I did care. Earth was in danger. I was the only one who could save it. And I didn't have the first idea how to begin.

Suddenly I felt very small, and very frightened.

I held out my hands and stared at them. They weren't big enough to hold the fate of the world.

CHAPTER TEN
THE ALIEN COUNCIL

After I sat for an hour or so without getting any ideas, I decided to look for Broxholm. Maybe he would help me.

Of course, for all I knew, he was one of the ones in favor of torching the planet.

But somehow I couldn't bring myself to believe that.

The problem was, where to find him? The *New Jersey* had thousands, maybe millions of rooms. It seemed like an impossible task, until it occurred to me that given what I had seen so far, it was likely the ship had a way to keep track of folks.

So I asked the URAT where Broxholm was.

Within seconds, I had an elevator code. I punched a few buttons, stepped through the wall, and found myself staring at Broxholm's back. This put me in the minority; everyone else in the room was staring at Broxholm's front.

"Everyone else" consisted of a group of eight aliens arranged in a half circle. Some were sitting, some standing. One dangled from the ceiling in a sling. Another was stretched across a rack that held up its purple tentacles. At the top of the rack a nozzle released a lavender mist that kept the tentacles moist and gleaming.

"We expect to reconnect with Kreeblim soon," said the alien in the rack. "She should be able to rewire one of the earthlings so that—"

The alien broke off when it noticed me. Broxholm, realizing that the alien was looking past him, turned to see what was going on.

"Peter!" he said sharply. "What are you doing here?"

"Looking for you," I whispered. I was frightened; it was clear I had stumbled into a place where I didn't belong.

The knobs on Broxholm's head began to throb. "Return to your room," he ordered. "I will be there directly."

I nodded and turned to go. But before I could leave, the tallest of the aliens, a huge sea-green creature who towered over even Broxholm, said, "Wait. As long as the child is here, let's talk with him a bit."

He looked around the semicircle of aliens. They all made gestures of agreement, which in this case ranged from a simple nod to a triple armpit fart.

"Tell us why you are here," said the alien with purple tentacles.

I thought for a moment before I answered.

"Because I believe the human race was born to go to the stars," I said at last. "It's what I've dreamed of since I was old enough to understand the idea."

"Tell us about your school," said another alien.

I did as he asked. The aliens listened carefully, making gestures of agreement, or interest, or annoyance. Sometimes they seemed astonished—sometimes astonished and disgusted, as when I described our basal readers.

"That will be enough for now," said the sea-green alien suddenly. "Thank you for your time."

"Wait for me in your room," said Broxholm, as I walked past him back toward the elevator.

I nodded, and continued toward the wall.

When I got back to the room, I was shaking. I don't like talking in front of people. It makes me nervous.

I was using the URAT to get a better understanding of the ship when Broxholm reappeared.

I had started by trying to find out why the ship was so huge. I couldn't believe they had sent something this big halfway across the galaxy just to drop a few spies on Earth.

It turns out that the method the aliens use for skipping over huge distances requires a kind of gravity distortion that can only be achieved with an enormous ship. In fact, the *New Jersey* was actually the smallest starship yet built.

The reason the loading dock was half empty was that the *New Jersey* had been dropping off smaller vessels here and there as it wandered through the galaxy. That was actually its main job: shuttling between stars, leaving a ship, or a dozen, one place, picking up new ships in the next. That, and carrying out the orders of the Interplanetary Council.

I was so engrossed in what I was reading that I actually jumped and shouted when Broxholm came through the wall.

"What's wrong?" he cried in alarm.

"Nothing," I said. "You just startled me."

Broxholm made a sign of understanding. "I suppose anyone living on a planet as violent as yours would need that kind of reflex reaction to stay alive."

Even though I had chosen to leave Earth, I was a little sick of hearing it get dumped on like this. "And what were you and your pals discussing?" I asked bitterly. "Some nice, nonviolent way to blow up the planet?"

It was Broxholm's turn to look startled. But he took it in stride. "That *is* one option being considered," he said calmly.

My stomach twisted at his words. Out here, so far from home, it was easier to remember the good things about Earth—things like Susan Simmons, dolphins, and chocolate chip cookies.

"How can you even consider something like that?" I asked, trying to fight back sudden, unexpected tears.

Broxholm gave his nose a pull. "I didn't say I was considering it. I said it was under consideration. Peter, you have to understand that the entire galaxy is in an uproar over this situation. We've been letting it ride for a while—we even got a break from making our decision because your planet's science got sidetracked a few decades ago. But the time is nearing when we must deal with what is known *across the stars* as 'The Earth Question.'"

"Why?"

"Because while they are not aware of it, your people are fast approaching the breakthrough point in space travel."

"You mean we're about to figure out how to go faster than light?" I whispered in awe.

Broxholm nodded. "We've been monitoring your science carefully. We know, better than you yourselves, how soon you will be able to come into space."

He paused, then crouched in front of me. Putting his hands on my shoulders, he looked directly into my eyes and said, "Do you understand what that means, Peter?"

I shook my head, feeling somewhat baffled.

"It means that for the first time in the 3,000-year history of the Interplanetary League, we are going to have to deal with a people who are at once smart enough to conquer space, and foolish enough to have wars. It means a peace that has lasted for 3,000 years, a peace that extends over 10,000 worlds, is in danger. Of course we are considering extreme measures. But the fate of Earth is by no means decided. The truth is, there are four main plans under consideration."

"What are they?" I asked, not entirely sure I wanted to know.

"One group believes we should take over your planet. A second thinks we should leave you on your own and see what happens; they believe you'll destroy yourselves before we ever have to worry about you. The third group wants to quarantine you—"

"What do you mean by 'quarantine'?" I interrupted.

"Cut you off from all connection with the greater galaxy," said Broxholm. "This could be done by setting up a space shield beyond which you could not pass, or by planting agents on Earth to sabotage your science, so that you could not learn how to get off the planet."

"That's terrible!" I cried, furious at the thought of anyone trying to bar us from space, from exploring the stars.

"I agree," said Broxholm. "But not as terrible as what might happen if you actually move into the galaxy at large. That is why one group simply wants to destroy the planet. They don't like the idea. But they think it is far better than letting you loose on the galaxy in your present condition."

"But why don't you just help us?" I cried, feeling scared and angry all at once.

Broxholm closed his orange eyes. "We don't know if we can. We believe there is something dangerously wrong with your people. This belief is based on three factors. First, the way you've

treated your planet. Second, the incredible violence you do to each other. Third—and this is the
really amazing thing to us—there's the condition
of your brains."

"Our brains?"

Broxholm pulled on his nose, then let it snap
back into place. "What baffles us most of all is the
fact that the human race has the most powerful brain
of any species in the galaxy."

CHAPTER ELEVEN
ANTHROPOLOGISTS FROM SPACE

I stared at Broxholm for a moment, then whacked the side of my head as if I thought my hearing had gone bad. "Say that again?" I asked.

"You heard me," he replied. "The human race has what may be the most powerful brain in the galaxy." He tapped one green finger against my forehead. "Trapped inside that skull is a brain that is the envy of every being on this ship."

"But I'm not smarter than the people here," I said—which was hard for me to admit, since being smart was the one thing I had always taken pride in. I paused, then added, "Am I?"

Broxholm shook his head. "No, you're not. But you *could* be. That's part of the mystery. The human brain is not only the most amazing piece of organic matter in the galaxy; it is also the *least used* brain in the known universe. We've never encountered anything like it—nowhere seen such a gap between what *could* be and what *is*."

As he talked, I began to get the feeling that Broxholm was actually jealous of the human brain.

"Do you have any idea what the rest of us could have accomplished if we had your brain?" he asked feverishly. "Any idea how it galls us to see that potential, and know how little you have done with it?"

I shook my head, too amazed to say a word.

"What terrifies us is what might happen if you learn to use your full intelligence *before* you become truly civilized. Stars above! If you people find your way into space before you fix whatever's wrong with your spirits, the damage you'd wreak could make what you've done to your own planet look like a forest rangers' picnic."

I sat back against the wall, staring at him. What could I say?

"Why do you think I was on your planet?" continued Broxholm. "What do you think was the point of trying to bring some of you back here for short-term study? We're trying to figure out why you act the way you do. We're looking for an answer—a cure, if you want to call it that."

He was pacing the floor now, not really angry, but agitated. It turned out that he had studied for years to make the trip to Earth. He was one of a group of aliens you might call "Anthropologists from Space"—a team watching the whole human race as if it was a tribe in the jungle.

A new question struck me. "If you guys are so wonderful, why were *you* so mean to our class?" I asked, remembering the way he had acted as a teacher.

Broxholm tugged on his nose. "For one thing, I am naturally gruff. Secondly, I would point out that you earthlings have a funny idea of what constitutes 'mean.' On my world we don't worry nearly so much as you people do about talking nicely to each other. We speak the truth and get on with things. On the other hand, we don't leave people to starve in the streets."

He paused, then added, "Actually, my natural gruffness was *not* the reason I behaved as I did with your class. I could easily have been as sweet and kind as anyone might have wished. However we were making a study of your learning styles—how you respond to different methods of education. We have an agent working in your town right now who is as 'nice' as I was nasty. It's all part of our study."

"You mean you're not really a creep?" I asked.

Broxholm stared at me. For a moment I was afraid he was going to be angry. But suddenly his nose began to twitch, just a little at first, then faster and harder, as if something inside was struggling to get out.

I realized that if he was an earthling, he would have been roaring with laughter.

"Peter," he said, "where I come from, I'm considered to be what you would call 'a real pussycat.' Look, young one, what was your greatest desire in all the world?"

"To see the stars!" I said, though suddenly I realized that my heart was saying something else.

87

I pushed the thought away. It was too frightening.

"To see the stars," said Broxholm. "Don't you think I knew that? Do you have any idea what trouble I caused myself by bringing you here?"

I shook my head.

He paused. "Nor need you know," he said at last. "Other than to understand that I chose to ignore a powerful command for two reasons. The first was that I owed you a favor for helping me escape *without having to hurt anyone.*"

I shivered as I realized just what Broxholm meant by that. "What was the second reason?" I whispered.

He spread his hands. "I like you," he said.

I blinked. Why was I starting to cry?

"Thank you," I whispered, feeling really stupid.

Broxholm put his arms around me. "You poor boy," he whispered. Then he stood and turned away. "Oh, you poor people," he said, so softly that I could barely hear him. "You poor, sad, wonderful people, so full of love and hate, hope and horror, sorrow and need."

He made a terrible, rasping sound, and suddenly I realized that he was weeping. Weeping for a planet that wasn't his, and all the pain that he had seen there.

I ran to him, threw my arms around him.

Then the two of us stood in the center of my room, and cried until we had no tears left.

CHAPTER TWELVE
HOW TO USE A URAT

So that was my first day on board the *New Jersey*. Is it any wonder I was exhausted?

Now you may have noticed that my "day" had started at night. But time on the ship was not related to time on Earth—or more specifically, time in Kennituck Falls. The ship had its own rhythm, and while there were times when more of its inhabitants were resting than others, in general it was busy twenty-seven hours a day.

According to Hoo-Lan, days on the ship were twenty-seven hours long because that was the schedule that made the most sense for the greatest number of beings on board.

Of course, since it was easy to control light and temperature, many of the aliens had private spaces to suit their personal needs. In some chambers the days were only ten hours long, and the temperature was like Death Valley during a heat wave. Some had long hot days, others had short cold days, and so on. Even so, everyone was able to function in the ship's main area—though it did mean that some of them had to wear thick layers of clothing, while others were nearly naked.

After Broxholm left that first "night," I used the URAT to get myself something to sleep in. The most interesting thing on the chart—at least, the most interesting thing that looked like I could actually sleep in it—was a kind of hammock device. The only problem was, I couldn't figure out where to hang it, since the walls in my room were smooth, and I had a feeling I wasn't supposed to put screws or nails in them, even if I had screws or nails, which I didn't.

I should have known not to worry. Each end of

the hammock had a rope. At the end of the rope was a ball. When you threw the ball at the ceiling, it stuck wherever it struck, and didn't come down until you gave the rope three sharp tugs.

So I got myself a hammock and hung it from my ceiling.

It was like sleeping on a cloud—though by the time I got it hung up, I was so exhausted I probably could have slept on a bed of cold seaweed and hot rocks.

I had no clock, so I don't know how long I had been asleep when I was awakened by a sudden loud buzzing.

"Who—what?" I sputtered. I tried to get up, but only succeeded in rocking the hammock sideways.

"It's not Hoo-Wat, it's Hoo-Lan," said an offended-sounding voice that seemed to come from nowhere. "May I come in?"

"I suppose so," I yawned, too groggy to think of just telling him to go away.

Almost instantly Hoo-Lan came walking through my wall. His blue shorts were covered with purple, red, and yellow flowers so bright that if I had still been asleep they probably would have woken me all by themselves.

"Ready to start your day?" asked Hoo-Lan cheerfully.

"I don't think so," I groaned.

"Tish-tush. We have too much to do for you to lie abed like this. Spit-spot, clip-clop, now's the time for all good men to come to the aid of their planet."

My grogginess vanished instantly. "Can you help me come to the aid of my planet?" I asked intently.

Hoo-Lan's big round nose twitched. "A figure of speech. I'm here to come to the aid of your brain. I'm your teacher, remember?"

I looked at him curiously. He stared back at me with huge, round eyes that almost dared me to read his mind. But of course I couldn't.

At least, not yet.

"First lesson," said Hoo-Lan, after I had found a bathroom and thrown some cold water on my face. "The uses of the URAT. You have already discovered some of them. I expect you would find many more on your own. But let's speed up the process."

"Fine with me," I said, settling into my wonderful chair.

"Right, then," said Hoo-Lan. "Now to begin with, the URAT is linked by microwave to the ship's main library. This means that it can find any kind of information almost instantly."

As it turned out, this also meant that the URAT could pull up fun stuff—plays and dances and concerts—from other worlds. If I wanted to go to the trouble, I could even hook it up to a holographic projector, which was truly amazing. Imagine being able to see a three-dimensional movie acted out in the middle of your living room—even a special effects extravaganza, with monsters, rocket battles, and alien landscapes. That's what this thing could do.

Next Hoo-Lan took me to the library itself, where they had machines you could actually plug yourself into so that you *experienced* stuff. These machines fooled all your senses; you didn't just see things—you tasted, touched, smelled, and heard them.

This was great for stories—though some of those alien stories were pretty weird, I want to tell you.

But it was even better for research.

Imagine your teacher has assigned a report on Columbus's first voyage. With one of these machines, you would feel like you were right on one of his ships; you would feel the sea breezes, smell the sailors' body odor, taste the kind of food they ate.

If you're a browser like me—the kind of person who starts out looking up horses and winds up reading about ancient Greece—doing research this way is incredible.

For example: say that while you're studying Columbus, you get interested in a bird you see flying by your ship. Whisper a command, and the bird is in your hands! It's like a three-dimensional illustration you can pick up and feel. And while you examine it, the machine pours information about it into your head.

Now let's say you wonder how the bird sees the world. Say the word and you're inside its skin and *you're flying!*

As you fly, you spot an island that looks interesting. Dropping down for a landing, you leave the bird's body behind, and begin to walk along the beach.

It's hot, so you decide to go for a swim. You *feel* the water—and taste it, too. And all the while you're really just in a room, plugged into one of these machines.

Let me tell you, a guy can get lost inside these things!

In fact, I guess that's sort of a problem. From what Hoo-Lan told me, when the machines were first invented, some beings got so fascinated by them that they never wanted to come out; a few got so involved in the machines they actually starved to death. So the ship's head librarian (who was purple and had twelve tentacles) had very strict rules about how long you could use the machines. She didn't want beings to get hooked.

Of course, I didn't learn all this stuff all at once. By the time Hoo-Lan was done showing me how to use the URAT that first day, I was pretty tired. I was also exhilarated, since the possibilities were so astonishing.

I was also depressed, because the more I saw

of the alien technology, the more clear it became that Earth didn't stand a chance if they decided to do us in.

I felt like the future of the planet was in my hands, which at the moment seemed awfully small and weak.

As it turned out, I was wrong. Earth's destiny wasn't so much in my hands. It was in my brain.

However, since I considered my brain my most precious possession, I wasn't entirely happy when the aliens asked if they could have it.

CHAPTER THIRTEEN
ALIENS WANT MY BRAIN

Actually, I suppose it would be more accurate to say that the aliens wanted to borrow my brain for a bit. I found out about it a couple of days after I had come on board the *New Jersey*. I had just climbed out of my hammock, and was getting ready to go order something to eat, when my URAT began to buzz.

Flipping it open, I saw Hoo-Lan. He looked upset. "Krepta, I need to speak to you. May I come to your room?"

"Could it wait until after I have something to eat?" I asked.

"Why don't I meet you in the dining area?" he replied.

That was fine with me. So we decided which dining area we would meet at—there were several thousand of them on board the ship. I punched the code into the transcendental elevator and stepped through the wall.

Hoo-Lan arrived in a pair of brilliant red shorts covered with tropical flowers and purple butterflies. We took a seat in a quiet corner.

"So what's up?" I asked.

Before he could answer, the alarm sounded, and we had to lie down on the floor while the ship made a leap across space.

"I wish they wouldn't always do that when I'm getting ready to eat," I groaned, when I was sitting at the table again.

"Someone did a study," replied Hoo-Lan. "It showed that, for no apparent reason, most jumps are made when the greatest number of beings are sitting down to eat." He punched a few buttons on the table, then looked up and added, "Sometimes the universe is just like that. By the way, did anyone tell you about the time component of the jumps?"

"Beg your pardon?" I asked, massaging my stomach and wondering if I would be able to eat or not.

"I take it that means 'No,'" said Hoo-Lan. A plate floated up from the center of the table. In the center was a pile of something that looked like marinated eyeballs.

I decided to skip breakfast. "Yes, it means no. Tell me about the time aspect."

"It's pretty simple, really. One thing that happens when we make one of those leaps across space is that while it takes only a minute of *our* time, the time passage in the outside world is quite a bit longer."

I wrinkled my brow. "I know that the faster we go, the slower time goes for us," I said.

I had learned that from all my science fiction reading. I knew that if we approached the speed of light, time inside the ship would come to a virtual standstill. This meant that if we spent a century traveling at the speed of light, those of us inside the ship would age by only a tiny fraction of that amount of time. But I had a feeling Hoo-Lan was saying something different.

"We're really not quite sure how it works," he confessed, when I asked him about it. "We just know that we start a space leap at one point, come out at another a few seconds later, and in the so-called real world, a whole lot of time has gone by."

"Wait a minute," I said. "How much time has gone by since I came on board?"

Hoo-Lan popped one of the eyeball-looking things into his mouth and bit down on it. The squishy sound made me wish we had decided to meet in my room instead.

"Can't say for sure," he said. "I don't always pay attention to that sort of thing. The ship travels at about half the speed of light most of the time. Between that and the space leaps we've taken, I'd guess that a month to a month and a half have gone by back on Earth."

I sat back in my chair, feeling slightly boggled. I had left on the 24th of May. From my point of view, about three days had gone by. But Susan Simmons might have done six weeks of living since then. It was weird: I was three days older and Susan was six weeks older. I wondered what it would feel like to go home and find that she was a grown up and I was still a kid.

I didn't care for the idea all that much.

I decided to change the subject. "What did you want to talk to me about?" I asked, looking at Hoo-Lan's plate and wondering if I wanted to try one of the things he was eating. I figured they couldn't possibly taste as bad as they looked.

Hoo-Lan poked at one of the things on his plate and a drop of green ooze came out.

I decided I didn't want to try them after all.

"I have been asked to get your reaction to an idea proposed by one of the members of the council that you broke in on the other day."

At first I was surprised that Hoo-Lan had heard about that incident. But if they had appointed him to be my tutor, I guess it made sense that they would keep him posted on what I was up to.

"What's the request?" I asked.

Hoo-Lan looked terribly uncomfortable. "You know the Interplanetary Council is engaged in a bitter struggle regarding what we are going to do about your planet. They would like your permission to tap your mind for some additional information."

"What do you mean, 'tap my mind'?"

Hoo-Lan ordered the table to take away the rest of his food. "First, they'll want to ask you a lot of questions. Then they'll probably hypnotize you, so that you can tell us things about your past that you have forgotten." He paused, then said, "Last of all, they'd like to do some brain work."

"Brain work?" I asked nervously.

"They're hoping if they dig around in there a bit, they may be able to find out what's wrong with you."

"What do you mean?" I yelped. "There's nothing wrong with me!"

Of course, that wasn't entirely true. I knew I was far from perfect. But I didn't think I needed brain surgery to fix my minor defects—or even my major ones.

"I don't mean you personally. I mean you earth-lings. We're wondering if the problem is organic."

"What problem?" I asked, knowing full well what he was talking about.

"The general human problem," said Hoo-Lan patiently. "Your race's willingness to destroy your home, kill each other, let people starve—all that stuff."

All that stuff indeed! Did they think they would find the reasons for all that in *my* brain?

Suddenly a horrible thought struck me: What if the reasons were in my brain?

I don't mean just my brain. I mean every human brain. What if the problem is that there's something wrong with the way we're wired? Would that mean the mess we've made of things isn't our fault? And if so, would that mean things were hopeless, that we could never fix the mess?

Or could the aliens do something about it? What if by looking inside my head, they could find a way to help us change? What if by examining my brain, they could learn how to help us stop wars forever?

Maybe it was no big deal. After all, CrocDoc had already done a little work on my head, and I had been able to get up and walk away from the table as if nothing had happened.

"Just how much digging do they want to do?" I asked.

"We're talking a total cut and paste job," said Hoo-Lan. "Most of the work would be done with light and magnets and atomic probes, of course. And our doctors are pretty good. But still, there's no guarantee."

I swallowed hard. "No guarantee of what?"

Hoo-Lan looked straight into my eyes. "No guarantee that you'll ever be able to think again," he whispered.

CHAPTER FOURTEEN
DISSECTED!

I stared at Hoo-Lan. A few minutes ago I was having a hard time trying to decide what to have for breakfast. Now I was supposed to decide if I was willing to risk my brain for the sake of the planet I had abandoned.

I sat without speaking for a long time. I thought about home and school. I wasn't particularly eager to become a drooling moron for the sake of Duncan Dougal. But then I thought about the things I had seen on the news—kids in the Middle East getting blown up, potbellied babies starving in Africa, street kids in South America being killed just to get them out of the way.

"You don't have to answer right away," said Hoo-Lan. "And we won't force you. You are one of us now."

"Am I really?" I whispered.

It was true that I was one of them in that they had accepted me, taken me in. But had I really let go of Earth? Or did I have my heart in the stars—and my feet in Kennituck Falls?

Hoo-Lan said nothing.

I stared at the table, then turned away from him. There was so much yet to see, to do, to explore. I had found my way to the stars. I was the one—the kid from Earth who had made it out into the galaxy. And now I was being asked to risk it all for the crazies I had left behind.

I rubbed the spot on my arm where Duncan used to punch me when he had had a bad night at home.

I thought of those kids in Africa.

"When do we start?" I whispered.

* * *

Broxholm came to see me later that day. "You don't have to do this, you know," he said.

"Do you think I shouldn't?" I asked.

He tugged on his nose. "I'm just worried about you," he said.

"I'm worried, too," I replied. "But hey, one reason I left Earth was that I figured no one would miss me. So what difference does it make?"

Broxholm looked at me for a moment. "I believe you overheard that we have a communications problem. My early departure from Earth left our other agent in Kennituck Falls without some essential equipment. So I cannot prove anything to you. But I believe that if I could show you the people back there, you would find some that miss you very much. Susan Simmons, for example."

I didn't say anything. I didn't like to talk about how I felt about Susan.

Our conversation was interrupted when Hoo-Lan stepped through the wall. He was wearing green shorts covered with hummingbirds.

"They're ready for you, Krepta," he said.

I touched foreheads with Broxholm, which is his planet's way of saying farewell with honor, and followed Hoo-Lan through the transcendental elevator to the operating room.

CrocDoc was waiting for us.

"Pleased to see you again, Krepta," he said soberly. His red jaws were drawn back in something that looked like a grin, but wasn't.

I nodded to him, and he made a gesture which translated into, "I salute your sinus cavities"— something I'm sure had more meaning for him than it did for me.

Having brain surgery on the *New Jersey* is not the same as having it on Earth. I wasn't scrubbed and put into a hospital gown. I almost wish I had been; some kind of ritual might have made me feel better, or helped me take it more seriously. Maybe it was just my fear that made me feel disconnected, as if I were moving through a dream of some kind.

Anyway, CrocDoc had me lie down on a table, told me the operation was being monitored by several dozen other doctors from a wealth of worlds, and then pricked me in the ear with something that immediately knocked me unconscious.

For a while, the sense of being in a dream increased. I felt like I was surrounded by mists, and trying to swim in molasses.

Voices seemed to whisper around me. Faces floated into my consciousness, some familiar, some totally unknown to me. Sometimes the familiar and the unfamiliar merged, or a face I had known all my life would stretch and pull into a strange new shape.

I saw Susan, Duncan, and Ms. Schwartz, and most of the other kids from school. If I could have thought about it, which I couldn't, I might have wondered if CrocDoc was touching nerves in my brain that were setting off specific memories— somehow tickling the areas where those images were stored.

I saw my father. He was crying.

I saw Duncan again. He was frightened. I tried to cry out, because I was sure that something had happened to him. Only I couldn't, of course, since I was sound asleep, with the top of my head off.

Then I saw a man, a tall man wearing a suit. He was sitting at a desk in what looked like a typical classroom. It was dark, as if he had been working late and never bothered to turn on the lights.

As far as I could tell, I had never seen him before.

In my vision, the man's face began to twist with emotion; I couldn't tell what emotion it was—it could have been fear, or anger, or sorrow, maybe some odd combination of all three. It was so intense, it was hard to label. But whatever it was, it slowly twisted his face until suddenly he shoved the desk forward so violently that it fell over, scattering the stuff on top all across the floor.

Standing, he strode across the room until he was facing the television set that sat on the far counter. His features still twisted with that unnameable emotion, he reached up and began to peel off his face.

The skin beneath the mask was blue. As he slowly pulled it upward, he revealed a huge white mustache, a comic nose, enormous eyes.

It was Hoo-Lan!

Trembling now, he raised his hand. The skin of the hand looked human, as if he was wearing a mask over that, too. But it began to glow, gently at first, then brighter and more intensely. As a howl that sounded like some unholy combination of pain and anger tore out of Hoo-Lan, a bolt of power surged from his fingertips and blasted the television set to pieces.

Then everything went black.

I wondered if I was dead.

CHAPTER FIFTEEN
BRAINS IN A BOTTLE

When I woke up, Hoo-Lan was staring at me anxiously.

"How did you do that?" he asked.

"Do what?" I asked, still feeling groggy.

"You were inside my head. I could feel it. I want to know how you did it."

I blinked. "I didn't even know I *did* did it," I mumbled, too confused to remember the dream I had had while I was unconscious.

I did notice that my words were slurred and slow. Was I all right? I couldn't tell.

"Peter, talk to me!" said Hoo-Lan urgently.

"Let the boy be," ordered CrocDoc. "He's been through a lot."

"Am I—did you—how did it go?" I asked, finally getting the words right.

"It's hard to say," replied CrocDoc, looking at me with his huge eyes. "We have to run an intense analysis on the data I uncovered. I did manage to get this," he said proudly, holding up a clear container.

Inside the container was a brain.

"My brain!" I screamed. "You took out my brain!"

I tried to grab for my head, but my hands were tied down.

"Well yes, but just for a while," said CrocDoc. "I'm going to put it back when I'm done."

I had tried to jump off the table when I first saw the bottle with my brain in it. That failed completely—either because I was tied down, or simply had no control over my muscles at the moment. Just as well, since it wouldn't have been a good idea for me to go running around without any brains. (Although I knew a lot of people back on Earth who did it all the time.)

I took a deep breath, trying to calm down. I took a lot of deep breaths before it did any good.

"How come I can see?" I whispered, when I thought I had some control over myself.

"Oh, your brain is still hooked into your head," said CrocDoc. Holding up the bottle again, he gestured to the bottom of it. "See all these wires? They run into your skull, providing nerve attachments. I'll unplug them whenever we're going to do some work that might be uncomfortable for you. But in the meantime, you can finally join us here in the world of the waking."

"Finally?" I murmured. "How long have I been unconscious?"

"About ten days, Earth time," said Hoo-Lan.

"More than a week!" I cried. "They haven't done anything to Earth yet, have they?"

"No, no. All action is postponed pending analysis of your brain."

Typical of my life. In most of the stories I've read, the fate of the world is in the hero's hands. In my case, the fate of the world was somewhere in my brains—maybe in my temporal lobes, or my corpus callosum, or my medulla oblongata. Wherever they finally found what they were looking for. Or didn't find it, since there was no guarantee that the answer *was* in my brain. Just a possibility.

A buzzer sounded from the ceiling. CrocDoc pushed a button. "What is it?" he asked.

"May we come in?"

I thought I recognized the voice, but I couldn't be certain, since I was still feeling kind of groggy. Would I ever feel alert again? Or was I doomed to a life of permanent mental fuzz?

The worst thing was, in my current condition, I didn't really care. I couldn't even *make* myself care. I wondered vaguely if this was what it was like to be hooked on drugs.

"Do you feel like having visitors?" asked Croc-Doc.

"Why not?" I said, though to tell you the truth, I really didn't care all that much at this point.

At once, Fleef and Gurk stepped through the wall.

"Oh, my," said Fleef, when she saw me strapped to the table, with my brain sitting on the counter next to me. Her face turned a deeper shade of orange, and the sphere on the stalk on her skull went "Neep! Neep!"

"How are you, Krepta?" asked Gurk. His big eyes seemed filled with worry.

"Okay, sort of," I said.

"We've been worried about you," said Fleef. "Everyone is very impressed with how brave you are."

"Does that mean you don't want to blow up Earth anymore?" I whispered.

"It means I hope we don't have to," replied Fleef, squeezing my hand.

I was disappointed. On the other hand, I suppose my being a good guy about all this didn't really reduce the possible menace of my planet. I sighed.

"We brought you something," said Gurk, trying to sound cheerful. He held up a bag. "Do you want to see?"

I tried to nod, but couldn't, because my head was strapped down. "Sure," I said. "Let's see."

He reached into the bag and pulled out a blob of fur.

"What is it?" I asked.

"It's a skimml," said Fleef. She sounded very pleased.

Gurk held the thing in front of my face. It was about six inches across, round and red—which made it look something like a big furry ladybug. After a moment two stalks rose out of the fur. The eyes on the ends of them looked at me and blinked.

"They're squishy." said Gurk. "And almost inde-structible. See?"

With that, he squeezed the skimml's middle, which caused it to bulge out of the top and bottom of his hand.

"Lots of fur, no bones," said Fleef.

Gurk set the skimml on my stomach. It walked up and took another look at my face, walked back to my stomach, turned around three times, and settled down with a sigh. After a moment it began to make a noise something like a window fan.

"It likes you!" cried Fleef happily.

I named the skimml Murgatroyd. It kept me company through the following days as CrocDoc turned my brain on and off while he examined it.

I had a lot of visitors. They all seemed to like to squeeze the skimml.

Broxholm showed up almost every day, as did Fleef and Gurk. Aliens I had never seen before stopped in to say hello. The crystal captain sent me a plant whose blossoms made singing noises that reminded me of my interview in the diamond chamber. And Hoo-Lan spent hours with me every day, telling me wonderful stories about the history of the galaxy.

Every once in a while he would look at me strangely, and ask me questions about what had happened to me while I was having the operation. But CrocDoc was always there, and wouldn't let him question me too sharply.

Finally the day came when CrocDoc was going to put my brain back in my head.

"Did you find what you needed?" I asked, still feeling groggy and disconnected.

His snout drooped down. "Not yet," he said. "But we're still analyzing the data. Don't despair, Krepta. All is not lost."

And then he put me to sleep.

* * *

When I woke up, the skimml was whirring on my stomach, and my brain was back in my head. Croc-Doc was leaning over me, just as he had that first day, after he had put in the language implant.

"Am I all right?" I whispered.

"With any luck, you'll be better than ever," he said.

I opened and closed my eyes a few times, and looked around the room. My vision was sharp and clear. I stretched, and realized that my hands were no longer tied down.

"Can I stand up?" I asked.

"No reason not to," said CrocDoc. "Just take it easy."

"Why don't you come up here?" I said, lifting Murgatroyd from my stomach to my shoulder. Murgatroyd snuggled in as I sat up and swung my legs over the edge of the table.

"Careful," said CrocDoc.

I waited a moment before standing up. But I felt terrific. It was as if my brain had been wrapped in fog, and now the fog was gone.

CrocDoc made a gesture that meant "I put my hand beneath your grandmother's egg," and told me how much he appreciated my help. "You may come and talk to me any time about our findings," he said. "I owe you that courtesy at least."

I gathered my things, the little gifts that aliens had brought me, squeezed Murgatroyd for luck, and prepared to return to my room.

But when I stepped through the transcendental elevator, it spit me out into a place I had never seen before.

CHAPTER SIXTEEN
DUNCAN

I was in a chamber filled with machinery. I recognized some of the devices as things the aliens used for communicating across space.

To my right was a kind of desk. Sitting on the desk was a helmet.

"Put it on," said a voice behind me.

I jumped in surprise, which caused Murgatroyd to squeak in protest. "Hoo-Lan," I snapped, spinning to face him. "Don't do things like that to me."

"Sorry," said the little alien. "I keep forgetting how skittish you are."

"I assume you're the one who brought me here."

Hoo-Lan reached out for the skimml. I handed it to him. "You assume correctly," he said, kneading the red ball of fur between his hands until Murgatroyd began to thrum with contentment.

"Would you mind telling me why?"

"Put on the helmet," replied Hoo-Lan.

I looked at the helmet nervously. "Is it safe?" I asked. As soon as the words were out of my mouth I thought, *Well, that was a stupid question, Peter. He won't tell me if it's not, so why bother to ask?*

But Hoo-Lan spread his hands and said, "No, not entirely."—Which just goes to show how much I knew.

"Then why do you want me to put it on? Haven't I taken enough risks already?"

"I ask because the possible benefit outweighs the risk," said Hoo-Lan. "Put it on."

I hesitated, then sat down at the table and put on the helmet. At Hoo-Lan's direction, I moved a couple of the control balls on the table in front of me.

And then I was inside Duncan Dougal's head. I shouted so loud that the skimml squawked and jumped out of Hoo-Lan's hands. It lay flat on the floor, stretched out and shivering, its eye stalks shooting up and down as it looked for trouble.

"For heaven's sakes, be quiet!" hissed Hoo-Lan, bending down to pick up Murgatroyd.

At least, I think that's what he said. I was too enmeshed in what was happening inside my head to pay attention to him.

I'm not sure how I knew that I was inside Duncan's head so quickly. It's not like there were any labels saying: THIS IS DUNCAN DOUGAL'S BRAIN.

Maybe I knew just because it *was* Duncan's brain, and his identity was stamped on every cell and synapse.

I felt uncomfortable about this. Little as I liked Duncan, I didn't think I had any right to poke around inside his brain. *Duncan,* I thought. *Duncan, can you hear me?*

No answer; either he wasn't aware of me, or wasn't able to answer, or was answering and it wasn't coming through.

Things happen fast inside a human brain. I started looking around. In a matter of seconds— or less, maybe; I don't know exactly how long it took—I had learned more about Duncan Dougal's life than I ever wanted to know.

Speaking from my point of view, here are some of the most important things I learned:

1) Part of the reason Duncan was such a beast was the way he got whacked around at home.

2) He was incredibly intelligent (this totally astonished me, until I found out more about it).

3) He was a sadder person than I ever would have guessed and

4) He had talked with my father not long ago, and my father was terribly upset about my leaving. Believe me, that last one was a shock to me.

Duncan, I thought again, *can you hear me?*

Still no answer. I took one last, quick look around the inside of his head, then raised the helmet from my own head.

Hoo-Lan was looking at me eagerly.

"What is going on here?" I hissed.

"You mean you got through?" he whispered. His voice sounded almost hungry.

"What is going on?" I asked again, tired of giving more answers than I got.

But Hoo-Lan wasn't ready to explain yet. Instead, he looked at me for a long moment, then answered my question with another question. Namely, "How would you like to visit another planet?"

I knew he was changing the subject, but I couldn't help myself. "When can we go?" I asked eagerly.

"How about now?" Passing Murgatroyd back to me, he led me to a circle printed on the floor. "Stand here," he ordered. "And as you value your life—don't move!"

He crossed the room and fiddled with some dials, then crossed back and positioned himself next to me. Almost instantly a blue beam shone down from the ceiling, and the room faded from sight.

When I opened my eyes, I was on a tiny bit of sand in the middle of a huge body of water.

It was night, and the sky above us was unlike anything I had ever seen—a vast sheet of black filled with stars. All right, that's not so weird. But their patterns were unfamiliar, and their light was so bright you could read by it. In the sky to our right floated a small green moon. A ribbon of shimmering, changing color stretched from horizon to horizon.

"All right!" I shrieked.

"Shhh!" said Hoo-Lan. "There are some very big animals around here. We don't want to attract their attention if we can avoid it."

I squeezed Murgatroyd and looked around nervously. I couldn't see any big animals. But who knew what form they might take here? For all I knew, the island we were standing on was actually some enormous sea creature. I looked down, half expecting to see a huge mouth in the sand.

"How did we get here?" I whispered.

"We took a ship-to-surface elevator," said Hoo-Lan. "It's like moving around inside the ship, but on a grander scale."

"Why didn't Broxholm use one of these when he came to Earth?" I asked, remembering our trip from Kennituck Falls to the *New Jersey*.

"Because first you have to set them up," said Hoo-Lan.

"Why would anybody set one up out here in the middle of nowhere?"

"I set it up, to be a private place. I like to come here to think."

I glanced at Hoo-Lan, who was easy to see because he was glowing again. "Who are you?" I asked.

"Your teacher," he said, as if that answered every-thing. "And as your teacher, I want you to see some things here."

He pulled a thin tube out of one of his pockets and blew a little tune on it. A moment later I heard the tune repeated somewhere across the water, as if it were being sung by a bird—or, for all I knew, some strange kind of fish. Or something else altogether, for that matter.

I turned to Hoo-Lan. He put his fingers to his lips and motioned me to silence.

We waited. The tune was repeated again, off in another direction, and then again, and again. Sud-denly I saw a commotion in the water, as something bright and huge rose from the depths to the edge of the island.

"Our chariot arrives," said Hoo-Lan.

My eyes were fixated on the green thing waiting just beneath the surface of the water. It was at least a hundred feet long. If it was a chariot, it was a strange one, because it was clearly a living animal—either that, or a very good imitation of one.

Hoo-Lan played another little tune. The creature rose to the surface and tipped back its head, which was the size of a small room. Its huge silver tongue extended to the shore like a gangplank.

"Go ahead," said Hoo-Lan. "Step aboard!"

CHAPTER SEVENTEEN

RHOOMBA RIDE, HOO-LAN'S HOME

Have you ever walked on a tongue? It's an odd feeling. The surface is firm but squishy, and it's a little hard to keep your balance.

I glanced behind me, to make sure Hoo-Lan was coming. Not that I didn't trust him. But walking into a mouth is pretty scary.

He nodded to me.

Clutching Murgatroyd, I walked on.

Hoo-Lan caught up with me as I reached the creature's teeth. They were taller than me, and made me think of huge icicles. Once we were clear of its fangs, the beast drew in its tongue, pulling us so far into its mouth that I was afraid we were going to be swallowed after all. Then it closed its mouth, and for a moment we *were* swallowed—by darkness.

That ended when Hoo-Lan began to glow. The blue light reflecting off the beast's silvery tongue made everything look strange and ghostly.

"Where are we going?" I whispered. Not that I thought the beast would hear us. It was just one of those places that made you want to whisper.

"We're going to my home," Hoo-Lan replied. He looked happy.

"Are we going across the water—or under it?"

"Oh, under. Definitely under. Rhoombas don't like to go on top of the water if they can help it."

"Rhoombas?"

"That's what you're riding in now," said Hoo-Lan. "They're one of the best ways to get around on this world."

"Do they ever, well—you know, do they have *accidents*?" I asked. I couldn't quite bring myself to come right out and ask if they ever made a mistake and swallowed their passengers.

"No one's perfect," said Hoo-Lan with a shrug.

I realized he was speaking in English again.

"Why are you doing that?"

"What did you see inside my head?"

I looked at him for a moment. "What do you mean?"

"I mean if you tell me what you saw, I'll tell you why I'm speaking English."

I hesitated, for two reasons. First, I wasn't sure just what I *had* seen when I was in Hoo-Lan's head; I needed a moment to think about it. Second, any time someone wants to know something *that* badly it makes me a little nervous.

"I've spent a lot of time studying the Earth," said Hoo-Lan, still in English. "Fascinating place."

Something Broxholm had said when I first came onto the spaceship floated to the top of my memory. "Hoo-Lan, did you name the *New Jersey?*"

"You get a cigar for that one," he said, putting his finger beside his nose.

"Who are you?" I asked, for the third time since I had known him.

"All take and no give makes for a lopsided friendship. Tell me what you saw in my head."

I closed my eyes and thought for a moment. "You were in a classroom. Only you didn't look like yourself. You were in disguise—sort of the way Broxholm was, when he took over our class. It was night. You were angry about something, angry enough that you began to glow until it was so bright it showed right through your mask. So angry you blew up a TV set."

He stared at me with a look that was something like horror. "Have you told this to anyone else?"

I shook my head.

"Please don't."

"Did it really happen?" I asked.

Before he could answer, a low, groaning sound rumbled around us. "Ah, we've arrived," said Hoo-Lan. "We'll talk more about this later."

"Arrived where?"

"At the city under the sea."

"But how are we supposed to get out?" I cried.

I didn't mind getting wet, but I knew if we were deep enough, the water pressure would crush us.

"Step back here," answered Hoo-Lan, leading me farther into the Rhoomba's throat. After we had gone about ten feet we came to a kind of chamber, a round area that went straight up.

Once Hoo-Lan was sure I was standing in the right place, he slapped the wall of the chamber three times. The Rhoomba roared and a mighty gust of wind sent us flying straight up, as if we were being shot through a whale's blowhole.

I landed on a padded surface, inside a small room. I was still trying to recover from the surprise when I saw a being who resembled Hoo-Lan drop something down the Rhoomba's blowhole, which was pressed against an opening in the floor. You could see the Rhoomba's leathery green flesh all around the edges.

"Reward," said the stranger, when he saw my questioning look. Then he drew a trapdoor shut across the opening, sealing off the little room.

No sooner was the trapdoor shut than a door in the side of the room opened and three more beings who were clearly of Hoo-Lan's race came running into the room. They wore light green togas, not brightly colored shorts. One by one, they clapped Hoo-Lan on the back, then gave him a big hug.

When they were done greeting Hoo-Lan, they turned to me and cried "Welcome, Krepta!"

"Thank you," I said, feeling a little shy.

Clutching Murgatroyd for comfort, I followed them out of the little room, still wishing Hoo-Lan had finished telling me why he was so wound up about what I had seen inside his head.

My questions faded when I passed through the door of the little room and found myself standing in the center of a great city of tree-lined streets, soaring buildings, and busy markets.

Something about the city struck me as odd. It took me a few minutes to figure out that the place had almost no sharp edges. The buildings, even the tallest ones, were smooth and rounded, and had a soft, almost gentle look. Some of them were covered with decorations. I don't know what they were made of, but the colors were mostly soft shades of blue and green and yellow, with here and there a deeper, stronger color that kept things interesting.

Even more striking than the buildings was the fact that the city was completely encased in a clear dome that stretched far above the top of the tallest building that I could see.

On the other side of the dome, above and all around the city, was water.

"Hoo-Lan," I whispered. "It's wonderful!"

"I'm glad you like it," he said, patting a six-legged animal that happened to be walking by. "I'm very proud of it."

We spent the whole day touring the city. It was beyond anything I had ever imagined. The rhoomba that delivered us was typical of the way things worked here; much of what needed to be done was taken care of by animals that had been trained and bred to the task. My favorites were the trash munchers. Every home and store had one—a fat little beast that loved to eat all kinds of garbage.

"Cuts down on the mess," said the little blue woman who first explained them to me.

All the animals seemed happy and well cared for.

All the people did, too.

After a while I began to get suspicious. I knew enough about cities to feel like something was missing.

"Don't you have anyone hungry here, anyone without a home?" I asked at last.

"Why should we?"

"I don't think you *should*," I said. "I just didn't know there could be a city without people like that."

"There can't, on your planet. The difference is that we've made a decision that it's not going to be that way. There's enough to go around, you know. Enough here, and enough on Earth. It's not like people *have* to be cold and hungry. You just haven't decided it's a bad idea."

"Of course we think it's a bad idea!"

"No, you *think* you think it's a bad idea. If your people, all your people, really believed it was a bad idea, they would stop talking about it and change things so it didn't happen anymore."

I squeezed Murgatroyd, trying to keep from getting angry about what Hoo-Lan had said. I had a feeling he was blaming me, personally, for everything that was wrong on Earth.

We had this argument outside a huge building.

"Come on," said Hoo-Lan. "There's something in here I want to show you."

137

People in the building greeted him as if he were an old friend. That was nothing surprising; it had been happening all day. One of the weirder things about the visit was the feeling I got that the whole city knew my teacher.

A series of long, snakelike creatures lifted us from floor to floor, until we were near the top of the building. On every floor, people shouted greetings to Hoo-Lan.

"Who are you?" I asked again, when we were standing outside a door on the top floor of the building.

Hoo-Lan smiled. "Why don't you look into my brain and find out?"

CHAPTER EIGHTEEN

CONTACT!

Hoo-Lan led me into a room filled with all sorts of fascinating equipment.

"You know," he said, as he began tinkering with some machinery, "I've spent a good part of my life trying to crack the secrets of telepathy."

"You mean direct communication from one mind to another?" I asked.

He nodded. "The thing is," he continued, staring at me intently, "*you've* got it. You went into my brain while you were being operated on and pulled out images. Jumbled ones, of course," he added hastily. "But you did pull them out of my head, and you did it without training. I think something that happened on the operating table helped unleash the ability in you."

He took the skimml from me and began squishing it back and forth. "You can't understand what this means, Krepta, unless you know that we've been trying for lifetimes to create this ability in some of our people. By *we*, I mean the Interplanetary League. The best we've been able to do so far is piggyback on thought transmission with some of our machines. That's the situation with your friend Duncan, by the way."

"He's not my friend!"

I regretted the words the instant they were out of my mouth. They made me sound small and petty. "What do you mean, anyway?" I asked, trying to cover up my stupid remark.

"Well, one of the early problems we had with star travel was that radio messages only move at the speed of light. Of course, this made it almost impossible to communicate between places that were light-years apart. We finally managed to invent a hyper-space transmitter, which gave us nearly instant contact between stars. Unfortunately, Broxholm had the only one on your planet. So when he was forced to flee, our remaining agent in Kennituck Falls, a female named Kreeblim, was left without a way to communicate with the ship after it had moved out of your solar system.

"To get around this, she used a brain enhancer on Duncan."

"You mean she made him smart?" I cried. That explained what I had found when I connected with Duncan back on the mother ship.

"No, she didn't *make* him smart," said Hoo-Lan. "She simply unleashed some of his basic potential. You humans are so much smarter than you act, it's appalling. Anyway, since thought is instant, by sending her messages through his brain, she is once more able to communicate with us."

"So what's the big deal about telepathy? Sounds like you already have it."

Hoo-Lan shook his head. "No," he said, passing Murgatroyd back to me. "It's not the same as direct mind-to-mind communication. *That's* what I'm after. That's what *you* managed when you tapped into my head. And when you got through to Duncan Dougal today, before we left the ship, you managed it without the brain treatments and mechanical connections we have to use for such a communication. Only three beings on the *New Jersey* could have made that connection. And each of them has had extensive training and repeated brain stimulation, and has to be *in* a force field with hardware attached to do it."

He looked at me. "But you—you did it without even trying. The secret is in there," he said, pointing at my forehead, which he was too short to reach. "Just like the reason for Earth's violence."

I was sick of everyone thinking I had all the answers. "This isn't the *Encyclopaedia Britannica*, you know," I said, tapping my head myself. (Though I must admit I'd read quite a bit of the *EB*.) Then another thought struck me. "You don't want to do more brain surgery on me, do you?" I asked, taking a step backward.

Hoo-Lan took my hand. "I just want to see if we can talk to each other," he said, leading me to a machine that looked like the one I had seen in the communication room on the ship.

"You stand here," said Hoo-Lan, positioning me under a metallic pyramid. "And I'll sit over here, where I can get some readings on what's going on inside your head. If you make contact, try using these dials to fine tune things. If things get too intense, punch this escape button."

The whole thing had happened so fast I didn't have time to think about whether or not I wanted to do it. I clutched Murgatroyd, feeling frightened and hopeful at the same time.

Hoo-Lan turned on the machine and said, "Now concentrate! Try to read my mind!"

I did as he asked. But instead of connecting with Hoo-Lan, I found myself back in contact with Duncan!

I couldn't believe it. Light-years away from Earth, visiting a distant planet, and who do I end up in a psychic link with? Duncan Dougal!

I mean, gimme a break, folks.

Duncan wasn't much happier than I was, though he didn't know I was there yet. Actually, he was feeling something that I had felt more than once since this all started: unhappiness that other worlds had been watching us as we bumbled along, blowing each other up and starving ourselves when there was enough food for everyone. *It's embarrassing*, he told himself.

It certainly is, I thought at him.

This time he heard me! I knew, because I was so linked to him that I could tell he wondered if he was losing his mind. *Who is that?* he thought.

Come on, Duncan—don't you know who I am?

Peter? he thought in astonishment. *Peter Thompson?*

None other! Wait, let me try something here. I fiddled with the dials Hoo-Lan had showed me.

Where are you? asked Duncan.

Shhh! Wait!

He was bursting with curiosity. But he waited while I tinkered with the machine, which was a little like adjusting the antenna on a television set. Suddenly I got complete focus: not only was I inside Duncan's brain, but Duncan was inside *my* brain.

To tell you the truth, I wasn't sure I liked the idea. I mean, in the past about the only way Duncan had communicated with me was through noogies and black eyes. But here we were, worlds apart, linked solely by our minds. So it was pretty exciting, even if it *was* Duncan. I could hear his thoughts as clearly as if he were speaking to me, instead of merely thinking.

"Where are you?" he asked.

"In space, silly. Where did you expect I would be? Oh, Duncan, it's glorious. The stars! I can't tell you. But it's frightening, too. There's a lot going on. Big things. And Earth is right in the middle of it. *We're* right in the middle of it."

"What do you mean?"

"The Interplanetary Council—that's sort of a galaxywide United Nations—is trying to figure out what to do about us. We've got their tails in a tizzy because our planet is so weird. From what Broxholm has told me—"

"Wait!" he replied. "Tell me about Broxholm. Is he treating you all right?"

"Well, that's kind of weird, too," I said. "I'm never quite sure what's going on with him. But listen, I've got to tell you this stuff first, because I'm not sure how long I can stay on, and you have to get word out to someone. Here's the deal. The aliens are having a big debate among themselves about how to handle the Earth. And I don't mean just Broxholm's gang. We're talking about hundreds of different planets here. As near as I can make out, they've narrowed it down to four basic approaches. One group wants to take over Earth, one group wants to leave us on our own, one group wants to blow the planet to smithereens, and one group wants to set up a blockade."

"*What?*"

"They say it's for the sake of the rest of the galaxy. They seem to find us pretty scary, Duncan."

"I don't get it."

"Don't ask me to explain how an alien's mind works," I snapped. "As far as I can make out, they think there's something wrong with us. Well, two things, actually. The first is the way we handle things down there. That's why they've been sending in people like Broxholm; they're supposed to study us and figure out why we act the way we do."

"So Broxholm was some kind of anthropologist—?"

"You could put it that way," I replied. I was astonished Duncan knew the word, until I remembered what had happened to him. "Anyway, the other thing that has them concerned is how smart we could be if we ever got our act together. Broxholm actually seems jealous. Every once in a while he goes on about the human brain being the most underused tool in the galaxy. I get the impression they're afraid if we learn to use our full intelligence before we get civilized—"

"We're civilized!" cried Duncan in indignation.

"Not by their standards. Anyway, they're afraid—"

I didn't finish the sentence. Someone had entered the chamber. I heard a lot of scuffling and squawking.

"Uh-oh," I said. "Something's happening. I gotta go, Duncan."

I pushed the escape button. Only I wished I hadn't, because the sight that greeted me when I came out of my trance nearly broke my heart.

CHAPTER NINETEEN
THE FADING GLOW

Hoo-Lan lay on the floor, stretched out straight and stiff as a board. Several of the little blue people were gathered around him, squawking in dismay.

"What is it?" I cried, rushing over to him. "What's happened?"

"The leader!" cried a green-haired woman. "What have you done to the leader?"

"It was the machine!" cried one of the men. "He knew he shouldn't use the machine!"

"No, it's not the machine," another one shouted. "It's him. It's the earthling!"

"What do you mean?" I asked. "What's wrong with Hoo-Lan?"

Before anyone could answer, the room was filled with a loud buzzing sound. It took me a moment to realize that the noise was coming from both Hoo-Lan's URAT and mine.

"The ship!" cried one of the men. "The ship is leaving. You must get him back to the ship!"

"But he's sick!" I said, nearly sick with fear myself.

"Yes. But he must be on the ship. Besides, his doctor is there. You must go back to the ship."

Gathering around Hoo-Lan's stiff body, the blue men and women picked him up and carried him to the room next door. The buzzing of the URAT grew more urgent.

"Stand here!" said one of the women, motioning to a circle on the floor. "Stand here!"

They put Hoo-Lan next to me. The men were pulling on their mustaches—a sign, my translator told me, of extreme grief.

"But what happened to him—?"

My words were cut off as a beam of blue light shot down from the ceiling, and we were sucked out of the city beneath the sea, through space, and back into the *New Jersey*.

I blinked. We were back in the room where we had started. "Hoo-Lan!" I cried, kneeling beside him. "Hoo-Lan, talk to me!"

He said nothing, only groaned a little. He was glowing, but only faintly.

Suddenly the alarm sounded. The ship was about to make a jump. I threw myself on the floor beside Hoo-Lan. Clutching Murgatroyd, who was chittering in alarm, I braced myself for the jump— and hoped that Hoo-Lan would live through it.

The horrible, high-pitched whine tore through the room, drowning my own moans of nausea. The tearing feelings began, became unbearable, and then ended. I lay next to Hoo-Lan, trembling and trying to recover, wondering how many light-years we had jumped, where we were now.

When I could push myself to my knees, I stared at Hoo-Lan. His glow was even fainter than before. I knew that he was dying.

I grabbed my URAT. "Give me the code for CrocDoc!" I cried. The moment the colored dots began to flash on the screen I raced across the room and punched the destination into the elevator. Then I ran back and tried to pick up Hoo-Lan. He was heavier than I thought, and his body was rigid, but I finally managed to get him into my arms.

Worried that I wouldn't get back across the room before the elevator did an automatic shut-off, I struggled toward the wall. The shut-off alarm sounded just as I pitched forward, falling through the wall and into CrocDoc's office.

Only CrocDoc wasn't there.

"Find him!" I shouted at the URAT. "Find Croc-Doc."

The machine gave me another code. Leaving Hoo-Lan on the floor, I hurtled through the wall. Interrupting a meeting of some sort, I grabbed Croc-Doc by the arm and said, "Your office! Quickly!"

To my relief, he didn't try to brush me off; instead, he immediately followed me back through the wall to his office.

I slumped against the wall in relief. I had done what I could do. Or so I thought. CrocDoc asked me to help him get Hoo-Lan onto the table. He was examining him while I watched in fascinated horror when Broxholm's voice came from the ceiling.

"Peter, you are wanted in the Council Room. The elevator is programmed. Please step through the wall."

"But, Broxholm—"

"Come at once!"

"Better go," said CrocDoc. "I'll take care of things here."

"But is he—will he—?"

"I make no guarantees," said CrocDoc. "However I believe he will still be here when you get back."

Be here? What did that mean? Still on the table, but dead as a tubeless television? I started to say something, but Broxholm's voice thundered through the speaker.

"Now, Peter!"

"Best go," whispered CrocDoc.

I went.

Broxholm was waiting for me when I entered the chamber. So was the rest of the alien council, the eight beings I had encountered the first time I entered this room.

"Peter Thompson—Krepta—Child of the Stars—" said the sea-green alien. "The time is fast approaching when we will make a decision regarding the fate of the Earth."

I considered bolting right then, racing off to the communication room to see if I could get one last message off to Duncan, somehow get him to warn the government, someone, anyone, who might be able to do something. Then at least the Earth might have a fighting chance.

"We offer you a chance to speak in Earth's defense," said the alien who hung on the rack. "Tell us something we do not know, something that might give us cause to think again as we deliberate."

"You need to ask someone else," I said desperately. "I'm only a kid! What can I tell you?"

"Then you refuse to speak on behalf of the planet?" asked the purple alien.

"No! That's not what I mean! I just don't know what to say. I haven't lived enough, seen enough. I know there must be more good things out there than I have seen, things worth saving, things too wonderful too lose. *I know it!*"

"Yet you chose to leave," said one of the aliens who had not spoken before this, a dark creature who looked more like a shadow than anything real and solid.

"I chose to leave, not to destroy it," I said.

"All leaving involves a kind of destruction," said the shadow. "The chick destroys the egg in hatching. No home is the same once someone has gone from it."

"Why don't you help us?" I cried. "You have answers, you can fix things."

"You don't need our answers," said another alien. "Your problem is not shortage of food, or land. You live on one of the most blessed planets in the galaxy—or at least you used to, until you fouled it so. What could we offer you but technology? And what would you do with it but create new problems? The technology is not the problem. Hearts and minds, those are the problem."

"Send me back," I said, hardly able to believe the words were coming out of *my* mouth. "Let me find a reason for you. I won't run away. I'm not afraid for myself. But I don't want you to hurt my friends. I don't want you to hurt my father!"

I stopped, astonished at what I had just said.

"Leave us for a time," said the sea-green alien. "We need to deliberate."

I looked at Broxholm. He nodded.

I left the chamber.

CHAPTER TWENTY
HOO-LAN'S WISH

I didn't even program the elevator, since I figured the aliens would send me wherever they wanted me to go. Somewhat to my surprise, I found myself back at CrocDoc's.

Hoo-Lan lay on the table, rigid and unmoving, his glow dimmer than ever.

"How is he?" I whispered.

"Not good," said CrocDoc.

I stood for a moment, staring at my friend, my teacher. "Can I do anything for him?" I asked quietly.

"No."

"I'll be back," I said.

Moving quietly across the room, I instructed the URAT to send me back to the communication chamber where I had first made contact with Duncan. Glancing over my shoulder, feeling guilty for leaving, even though there was nothing I could do, I stepped through the wall.

What had happened to Hoo-Lan when he tried to make mental contact with me? Was this my fault? Was my human brain so poisonous it had done something terrible to his mind?

Once I reached the communication chamber, it took me a while to make contact with Duncan again. I wondered if he was still in the force field. After all, even though it had been only a couple of hours by my time since I spoke to him, the ship had made a space-shift since then. How much time had passed on Earth?

I fiddled with the controls, until I made contact with Duncan Dougal, my old enemy, my new ally. As I began to fine-tune the connection, it occurred to me that if this Kreeblim character they had mentioned had put Duncan in the force field, it might not be a good idea for me to say too much until I knew whether or not she was there.

"Duncan," I thought. "Is there anybody there?"

"Just you and me."

"Good." I finished focusing the connection, so we could see each other. "Listen, things are heating up out here. The aliens are planning something. I don't know what, but it's big. You have to get word to the government."

Duncan was explaining why he thought that was a stupid idea when we heard someone coming up the attic stairs.

"Pretend I'm not here," I said desperately. "I can't be caught talking to you like this. I'll try to hold on, but I'll break the connection if I have to."

"I understand," said Duncan.

But the person who showed up at the top of the stairs was no menace. Well, aside from the fact that the sight of her did something strange to my insides.

It was Susan Simmons, and I suddenly realized I had missed her more than I had guessed. I sighed. Why couldn't the aliens have hooked me into *her* brain?

With the URAT to help me, I told Susan how to free Duncan from the force field. Once she had him out, I was a little surprised to find that Duncan and I were still in contact.

When he said that he was surprised as well, I replied, "Of course. Your head is what we call wetware—an organic machine. At the moment, you happen to be one of the most powerful communication devices in the galaxy, Duncan. Now listen, I've got some important stuff to tell you. There are big things happening up here, and you need to—oh no!"

The last words came out as a shout of terror, because a pair of hands had just grabbed me by the back.

"You shouldn't do things like that, Peter," said Broxholm, turning me around and picking me up so that I had to stare straight into his huge orange eyes. "It makes it harder for us to trust you."

I wondered how much Broxholm had heard of what I had just told Duncan and Susan. Then I realized he couldn't have heard any of it, since it had all been done inside my head!

"The Council wants to see you again," said Broxholm. Carrying me across the room, he stepped through the transcendental elevator and back into the council chamber.

"What do you know about the fall of Hoo-Lan?" asked the sea-green alien, as soon as I was standing before the council again. He seemed sterner than ever, maybe even angry.

I hesitated. "He tried to connect himself to my mind," I said. "It happened to him then."

The other members of the council stirred restlessly. I got the sense I had said or done something wrong.

"Hoo-Lan was a fool," said the alien with purple tentacles.

Something inside me snapped. I had had enough of their superiority, their all-powerful lording it over me. I liked Hoo-Lan. No, I loved Hoo-Lan. He had been kind and gentle to me, taught me things, cared for me.

"Don't you say that!" I cried, rushing toward the alien.

I suppose it wasn't the best demonstration of how earthlings might be expected to control themselves. It didn't make any difference; I ran right through him without touching him.

I stopped, turned around, blinked in dismay.

I walked back toward the alien, waving my arms. They passed back and forth through his purple body.

"Broxholm!" I cried. "What's going on!"

He looked startled. "Did you really think they were here?" he asked. Then he blinked and said, "Do you realize who these beings are?"

"The people in charge of the ship?" I asked uncertainly.

Broxholm's nose twitched. The images of the other eight aliens responded with their various forms of laughter.

"These are the chief leaders of the Interplanetary Council," said Broxholm.

I ran back to his side, stunned at what he was saying. I had just tried to punch out one of the rulers of the galaxy!

For a kid who considers himself an intellectual, this was not the high point of my emotional life.

"What are they doing here?" I whispered. "Or not doing here?" I added, trying to salvage some dignity with a little humor.

"We generally meet via holographic projection," said a red alien, who looked sort of like a pile of sea-weed. "It is simplest that way, as it allows us to stay on our own planets, and yet remain in contact. That way, we can hold our meetings anywhere we wish."

"As to your defense of Hoo-Lan," said the purple alien I had tried to clobber, "the emotion is admirable even if your way of expressing it is deplorable—and totally typical of your kind."

For a moment I had a terrible feeling they were going to blow up the planet because I had lost my temper. That was more guilt than I wanted to deal with!

"However you misunderstand our relationship with your mentor. Hoo-Lan was once a *member* of this council. He chose to resign, to pursue other interests. We have the utmost respect for him. We merely think he is wrongheaded."

"He has sent us a message," said the shadow. "I fear it may be the last message we will ever have from him."

I felt a lump begin to form in my throat. Had being in touch with my brain killed him? Were the people of Earth *that* terrible?

"Ever so gloomy," said Red Seaweed to the shadow. "Hoo-Lan may yet rejoin us."

"May and may not," replied the shadow. "Nonetheless, while you know that I favor the destruction of the Earth, I am willing to hold back in favor of what may be Hoo-Lan's last request."

"What was his last request?" I asked, my voice trembling.

"That we perform one final study of the Earth before we make our decision," said the shadow. "Personally, I think this is an enormous waste of time. But out of respect for a fallen comrade, I accede to his wishes, which specifically call for you and Broxholm to return to Earth and, with the help of the agent who is already in place there, file a final report."

"Those in favor?" asked Sea-green.

The vote was unanimous.

CHAPTER TWENTY-ONE
HOME TO HOME

Once these aliens made up their minds, they weren't ones to dillydally. Within minutes Broxholm and I were riding a blue beam from the ship to the Earth.

One reason we could do that was that the last space-shift had brought us back into Earth orbit. The transporter beam only had a range of a few hundred thousand miles.

I think that the funniest thing I ever saw in my life was the look on Duncan's face when Broxholm and I shimmered into place in Kreeblim's attic.

That was the funniest thing. The most beautiful thing (I can't believe I'm saying this!) was Susan Simmons's face.

Of course, part of what made it so lovely to me was how glad she was to see me.

"Peter!" she cried, running over and throwing her arms around me.

I was a little embarrassed. "Hi, Susan," I said. "It's nice to see you."

Gak! "Nice to see you." How stupid! That was a tenth, a thousandth of what I *wanted* to say to her. Only I didn't know how—especially with everyone else around us.

Broxholm broke the awkwardness of the moment in his own stiff way. "Good evening, Miss Simmons, Mr. Dougal," he said, nodding his green head. "I can't say it is exactly a pleasure to see you again, but since we are going to be working together, I hope that we will be able to put the past behind us."

For Broxholm, it was a pretty gracious speech.

"Working together?" asked Susan.

"How would you like to save the Earth?" I asked, trying to sound casual and heroic.

We didn't give them much chance to answer,

to tell you the truth. Within minutes I led the way back to the takeoff position. Duncan positioned himself between me and Susan, which was annoying. I told myself to ignore it; from tapping into his brain, I knew what he had been through in the last month.

Of course, I had been through a lot myself.

The blue beam shimmered around us. We were dissolved into electrons and hurtled into space, then reformed inside the great alien ship that I had ridden to the stars.

Somewhere below us was the planet we had to save.

Somewhere below us was my father.

Somewhere in the ship was a little blue alien who had made a dying wish that the Earth would have a final chance.

We had to honor that, try with all our hearts to save the planet.

We had to honor him.

I hoped that somehow he would live, so that Susan and Duncan could meet him.

Seconds later Kreeblim and Broxholm arrived.

"You're lucky," I told Susan and Duncan. "Traveling by transport beam saves you a trip through the disinfecting process."

"Disinfecting?" asked Duncan, wrinkling his nose.

"I'll tell you all about it later."

"You can tell them now, if you want," said Broxholm. "Kreeblim and I must go in for a meeting with the Council. You'll have some time while we're gone."

With that, the two of them disappeared through the transcendental elevator.

"All right, Peter, give," said Susan.

"Beg pardon?" I asked innocently.

But you know all that part. I told her and Duncan the same story I've just told you.

About the time we were done, Broxholm and Kreeblim returned. "The Council will see you now," said Kreeblim, her nose waving in front of her.

Nervous, excited, terrified, we followed them through the transcendental elevator to the room where the images of eight aliens were waiting to give us our instructions.

There was something different about the

chamber this time. Floating in the center of it was a huge, holographic image of the earth. Think of the globe you have in your classroom. Now imagine it eight feet across, created in perfect detail.

I felt Susan's hand slip into mine. "It's so beautiful," she whispered.

I didn't say anything. From out in space, the planet *was* beautiful. But I knew what was happening back on the surface, what people were doing to each other.

What would happen to *us* when we went back down there? Could we find some way to convince the aliens not to destroy it?

Suddenly, I realized Duncan was standing close to me. To my surprise, he slipped his arm around my shoulder. "We can do it, Peter," he whispered.

I nodded, still staring at the image before us, the image of Earth, the planet I had abandoned, and now must try to save.

My home.

READ ON FOR MORE
OUT-OF-THIS-WORLD ADVENTURES
IN AN EXCERPT FROM BOOK FOUR:

MY TEACHER FLUNKED THE PLANET

Broxholm's orange eyes were glowing. The leathery, lime-green skin of his face was stretched tight in a look that I could not interpret. The viewscreen behind him showed an image of the Earth, floating in the dark glory of space.

Broxholm pointed to a red button that glowed more brightly than his eyes. "This is it," he said. "*The* button."

My throat was dry. "What would happen if you pushed it?"

His lipless mouth pulled back in something like a smile, revealing rounded, purplish teeth. "Nothing. At least, not now. It takes a complex series of secret commands to activate it."

"And if that series of commands is used?" asked Susan Simmons, who was standing beside me.

Broxholm turned and gazed at the image of Earth. "Stardust," he whispered.

"Whoa!" said Duncan Dougal. "Major bummer!"

Another being entered the chamber. Turning, I saw Kreeblim, the alien who had fried Duncan's brain and made him super-smart. Her lavender hair, thick as worms, was writhing around her head. "The council is ready to see us," she said, gesturing over her shoulder with her long, three-pronged nose.

I swallowed. The Interplanetary Council was trying to decide how to handle what they called "the Earth Question"—which was basically, "What do we do with the only species on ten thousand planets that is bright enough to figure out space travel, yet dumb enough to have wars?"

That species was human beings, of course, and I didn't much care for any of the aliens' current plans, which I had explained to Susan and Duncan earlier that night when I told them the story of my experiences since I had gone into space with Broxholm.

"If we start with the least nasty option and work up," I had said, "then Plan A calls for the aliens to leave us alone for now."

"That's not so bad!" Susan had said.

"Unfortunately, most of the aliens who favor it do so because they figure if they leave us alone, we'll destroy ourselves before we make it into space. That way the problem is solved, and they don't have to feel guilty."

"That *stinks!*" Duncan had cried.

"Agreed. Now, the aliens who support what we'll call Plan B would like to take over the planet."

Susan's eyes had widened. "An alien invasion, just like we feared from the beginning!"

"Not quite. This group wants to fix things. They would cure diseases, stop wars, end poverty, that kind of thing."

Duncan had blinked in surprise. "Sounds great!"

"It would be, except they'll only do it if we give them total control of the planet."

Duncan had started to ask why, then nodded.

"They're afraid once they give us their technology we'll use it against them."

"You've got it," I'd said, reminding myself not to be surprised when Duncan figured things out.

"So what's the third option?" Susan had asked.

"Plan C: restrict us to our own solar system, either by sabotaging our science so we never develop faster-than-light travel, or by setting up a military blockade."

Since I have always believed it is our destiny to go to the stars, I hated that idea more than I can tell you.

"Most aliens think that wouldn't work," I had continued. "They figure sooner or later we'd get out anyway. So we have Plan D—D for destruction, you might say. The group supporting this wants to blow us up now, before we can get into space and really make trouble. They believe if we make it out of the solar system, the final cost in lives and destruction will be *far* greater than if they simply wipe us out today. They look at us the way we would look at a group of monkeys that accidentally learned to make atomic bombs: interesting, but too dangerous to be allowed to live."

The bad news was, the aliens seemed to be leaning toward Plan D. The good news was, they were going to let us try to change their minds.

We followed Kreeblim to the wall. She had her pet poot—which was also *named* Poot, for reasons I didn't understand—riding on her shoulder. Poot was sort of an alien slug that oozed and changed shape. I had noticed that Duncan seemed to be very fond of it. I guess it was fond of Duncan, too, since when it noticed him it raised a blob of itself and cried, "Poot!"

Kreeblim stopped in front of a large circle. Mounted in the wall next to it were twelve rows of multicolored marbles. She punched six of the marbles. The circle turned blue.

This was what the aliens call a transcendental elevator. It could transport beings from one place to another instantly—which was just as well, since the *New Jersey* (that was the spaceship we were on) had thousands of miles of corridors.

I followed Kreeblim through the circle and into the meeting chamber of the Interplanetary Council.

Susan gasped when she came in behind me. I

didn't blame her. Each of the eight beings on the council came from a different world. Seeing them all together was plenty strange.

Actually, what we were *seeing* were holographic projections of the council members. The council members themselves remained on their own worlds. However, the three-dimensional images were so realistic, I rarely thought about that.

First to speak was an alien who looked like a pile of red seaweed with thick green stalks growing out of the top. It made a series of popping, bubbling sounds, then wiggled the squishy-looking pods that dangled from the end of each stalk to indicate that what it had said was a question.

I understood the gesture because the aliens had installed a Universal Translator in my brain, and it interpreted whatever any of them said. In turn, I was to translate their sounds (and gestures) for Susan and Duncan.

I turned to Susan. Her hair, usually blond, had a green tint from the odd light of the chamber. Susan is very pretty by Earth standards, but I had seen so many versions of beauty since I joined the aliens

I didn't think about that much now. "He wants to know if you understand why you are here," I said.

"I do," she replied, speaking directly to Red Seaweed. "Peter told me all about it."

"And do you accept this task?"

Susan took so long to answer that I began to fear that the alien might get upset. I understood; it was a big job. But even so . . . I gave her a nudge.

"I accept!" she said, more loudly than I expected.

"And you, Duncan Dougal?" asked an alien who looked more like a shadow than anything real and solid. It spoke by changing the way light reflected from its body.

Duncan's round face was serious. It was hard for me to imagine a kid who had bullied his way through grade school, a kid who appeared to have all the sensitivity of a brick, being responsible for the survival of the planet. But I was prejudiced. Duncan had been picking on me—and everyone else in our class—for so long that it was hard to remember how different he was now that the aliens had unleashed his natural intelligence by frying his brain.

When I translated the question, Duncan nodded. "I accept," he said solemnly.

"And you, Krepta?" asked a tall, sea-green alien.

I hesitated for only a moment. After all, the
mission had been partly my idea. "I accept," I said.
Though I meant to say it proudly, my voice came
out sounding small and scared.

Next to speak was a purple alien whose long
tentacles stretched across a silvery rack. A nozzle
mounted above the rack sprayed lavender mist over
the tentacles, keeping them slick and shiny.

"Broxholm ign Gnarx Erxxen xax Scradzz?" it
asked.

That mouthful of syllables represented Broxholm's full name, including his family group (Gnarx
Erxxen) and his planet (Scradzz). Broxholm was
standing behind me. I turned to look at him. Putting
a hand on my shoulder, he wrinkled his high, green
forehead—his way of signaling agreement.

The final member of our party to be sworn in
was Kreeblim. Her thick lavender hair was rippling
with so many conflicting emotions she looked as if
she had a colony of confused worms climbing out

of her head. I began to wonder if she had changed her mind. But after a moment she closed her third eye, the one in the middle of her forehead, and said, "I accept!"

The council didn't ask us to swear on a holy book or anything; the aliens expect that if you say you'll do something, you'll do it. Only I wasn't entirely sure what we had just said we would do.

Basically, they had given us the last three weeks of October to put together a report on the state of Earth and its people.

But what was supposed to be in the report? How could we make them think better of us? At the moment, the aliens viewed us the way you and I look at flu germs—insignificant, yet nasty and dangerous. Or worse. I think they considered all of humanity as a sickness threatening to overtake the galaxy if something wasn't done about us.

"The newcomers will need translators," said a large, batlike alien who dangled from the ceiling in a sling. Its voice, which I had not heard before, was like nails scraping over concrete. I could feel it in my spine.

After Susan and Duncan took their hands away from their ears, I translated the alien's screech. Duncan looked puzzled. "Why do we need translators to go back to Earth?"

"Because your planet, which has yet to figure out the benefit of true communication, has hundreds of different languages," screeched the batlike alien.

The other aliens made sounds of sorrow and disapproval at our backward ways.

When I explained Bat-thing's answer, Duncan's eyes lit up. "You mean these translators will let us understand any language on *Earth*?" he cried eagerly.

"They would hardly be Universal Translators if they didn't," said Red Seaweed, adding a gesture that meant something like, "Is water wet?"

"Wow!" said Duncan. "This is going to be great!" Suddenly his smile faded. The blood drained from his face. "Wait a minute," he said, his voice quavering. "Are you going to do brain surgery on me?"

In my opinion, brain surgery on the old Duncan would have been a good idea. He'd had nothing to lose, and it might have improved things. But now that I had been inside his brain a couple of times (as a result of being hooked into some alien communication machines), I understood why he was so upset. Since the aliens had fried the thing, it was pretty amazing. I wouldn't have wanted to take a chance with it, either.

I was trying to decide whether to tease Duncan or reassure him when a wave of dizziness swept over me. My own brain felt as if it had come loose inside my skull and begun to spin.

"Nikka, nikka, flexxim puspa!" I cried.

As I was wondering where the words had come from, everything went black, and I collapsed in a heap on the floor.